THE
STATISTICAL
PROBABILITY
OF LOVE AT
FIRST SIGHT

THE STATISTICAL PROBABILITY OF LOVE AT FIRST SIGHT

Jennifer E. Smith

poppy

Little, Brown and Company
New York   Boston

Copyright © 2012 by Jennifer E. Smith

Poppy

Hachette Book Group
237 Park Avenue, New York, NY 10017
For more of your favorite series and novels, visit our website at www.pickapoppy.com

Poppy is an imprint of Little, Brown and Company.
The Poppy name and logo are trademarks of Hachette Book Group, Inc.

The publisher is not responsible for websites (or their content)
that are not owned by the publisher.

First Paperback Edition: August 2012
First published in hardcover in January 2012 by Little, Brown and Company

Library of Congress Cataloging-in-Publication Data
Smith, Jennifer E.
The statistical probability of love at first sight / by Jennifer E. Smith. — 1st ed.
p. cm.
Summary: Hadley and Oliver fall in love on the flight from New York to London, but after a cinematic kiss they lose track of each other at the airport until fate brings them back together on a very momentous day.
ISBN 978-0-316-12238-2 (hc) / ISBN 978-0-316-12239-9 (pb)
[1. Love — Fiction.   2. Fate and fatalism — Fiction.   3. Air travel — Fiction.
4. Weddings — Fiction.   5. Funeral rites and ceremonies — Fiction.
6. Remarriage — Fiction.   7. London (England) — Fiction.]   I. Title.
PZ7.S65141St 2012
[Fic] — dc22   2010048704

10   9   8   7   6   5   4   3   2   1

RRD-C

Printed in the United States of America

For Kelly and Errol

"AND O THERE ARE DAYS IN THIS LIFE, WORTH LIFE AND WORTH DEATH."

— *Charles Dickens*

OUR MUTUAL FRIEND

PROLOGUE

There are so many ways it could have all turned out differently.

Imagine if she hadn't forgotten the book. She wouldn't have had to run back into the house while Mom waited outside with the car running, the engine setting loose a cloud of exhaust in the late-day heat.

Or before that, even: Imagine if she hadn't waited to try on her dress, so that she might have noticed earlier that the straps were too long, and Mom wouldn't have had to haul out her old sewing kit, turning the kitchen counter into an operating table as she attempted to save the poor lifeless swath of purple silk at the very last minute.

Or later: if she hadn't given herself a paper cut while

printing out her ticket, if she hadn't lost her phone charger, if there hadn't been traffic on the expressway to the airport. If they hadn't missed the exit, or if she hadn't fumbled the quarters for the toll, the coins rolling beneath the seat while the people in the cars behind them leaned hard on their horns.

If the wheel of her suitcase hadn't been off-kilter.

If she'd run just a bit faster to the gate.

Though maybe it wouldn't have mattered anyway.

Perhaps the day's collection of delays is beside the point, and if it hadn't been one of those things, it would have just been something else: the weather over the Atlantic, rain in London, storm clouds that hovered just an hour too long before getting on with their day. Hadley isn't a big believer in things like fate or destiny, but then, she's never been a big believer in the punctuality of the airline industry, either.

Who ever heard of a plane leaving on time anyhow?

She's never missed a flight before in her life. Not once.

But when she finally reaches the gate this evening, it's to find the attendants sealing the door and shutting down the computers. The clock above them says 6:48, and just beyond the window the plane sits like a hulking metal fortress; it's clear from the looks on the faces of those around her that nobody else is getting on that thing.

She's four minutes late, which doesn't seem like all that much when you think about it; it's a commercial break, the period between classes, the time it takes to cook a microwave meal. Four minutes is nothing. Every single day, in every single airport, there are people who make their flights at the very last moment, breathing hard as they stow their bags and then slumping into their seats with a sigh of relief as the plane launches itself skyward.

But not Hadley Sullivan, who lets her backpack slip from her hand as she stands at the window, watching the plane break away from the accordion-like ramp, its wings rotating as it heads toward the runway without her.

Across the ocean, her father is making one last toast, and the white-gloved hotel staff is polishing the silverware for tomorrow night's celebration. Behind her, the boy with a ticket for seat 18C on the next flight to London is eating a powdered doughnut, oblivious to the dusting of white on his blue shirt.

Hadley closes her eyes, just for a moment, and when she opens them again, the plane is gone.

Who would have guessed that four minutes could change everything?

1

Airports are torture chambers if you're claustrophobic.

It's not just the looming threat of the ride ahead—being stuffed into seats like sardines and then catapulted through the air in a narrow metal tube—but also the terminals themselves, the press of people, the blur and spin of the place, a dancing, dizzying hum, all motion and noise, all frenzy and clamor, and the whole thing sealed off by glass windows like some kind of monstrous ant farm.

This is just one of the many things that Hadley's trying not to think about as she stands helplessly before the ticket counter. The light outside is starting to disappear and her plane is now somewhere over the Atlantic, and she can feel something inside of her unraveling, like the slow release of air from a balloon. Part of it is the impending flight and part of it is the airport itself, but mostly—*mostly*—it's the realization that she'll now be late for the wedding she didn't even want to go to in the first place, and something about this miserable little twist of fate makes her feel like crying.

The gate attendants have gathered on the opposite side of the counter to frown at her with looks of great impatience. The screen behind them has already been switched to announce the next flight from JFK to Heathrow, which doesn't leave for more than three hours, and it's quickly becoming obvious that Hadley is the only thing standing between them and the end of their shift.

"I'm sorry, Miss," one of them says, the suppressed sigh evident in her voice. "There's nothing we can do but try to get you on the later flight."

Hadley nods glumly. She's spent the past few weeks secretly wishing this very thing might happen, though admittedly, her imagined scenarios have been a bit more dramatic: a massive airline strike; an epic hailstorm; an immobilizing case of the flu, or even the measles, that would prevent her from flying. All perfectly good reasons why she might have to miss her father's trip down the aisle to marry a woman she's never met.

But being four minutes late to your flight seems just a little too convenient, maybe a tad suspicious, and Hadley isn't at all sure that her parents—either of them—will understand that it wasn't her fault. In fact, she suspects this might fall onto the very short list of things they'd actually agree upon.

It had been her own idea to skip the rehearsal dinner and arrive in London the morning of the wedding instead. Hadley hasn't seen her father in more than a year, and she wasn't sure she could sit in a room with all the important people in his life—his friends and colleagues, the little world he's built around himself an ocean away—while they toasted to his health and happiness, the start of his new life. If it had been up to her, she wouldn't even be going to the wedding itself, but *that* had turned out to be nonnegotiable.

"He's still your dad," Mom kept reminding her, as if this were something Hadley might forget. "If you don't go, you'll regret it later. I know it's hard to imagine when you're seventeen, but trust me. One day you will."

Hadley isn't so sure.

The flight attendant is now working the keyboard of her computer with a kind of ferocious intensity, punching at the keys and snapping her gum. "You're in luck," she says, raising her hands with a little flourish. "I can get you on the ten twenty-four. Seat eighteen-A. By the window."

Hadley's almost afraid to pose the question, but she asks it anyway: "What time does it get in?"

"Nine fifty-four," the attendant says. "Tomorrow morning."

Hadley pictures the delicate calligraphy on the thick ivory wedding invitation, which has been sitting on her dresser for months now. The ceremony will begin tomorrow at noon, which means that if everything goes according to schedule—the flight and then customs, the taxis and the traffic, the timing all perfectly choreographed—she'll still have a chance at making it on time. But just barely.

"Boarding will start from this gate at nine forty-five," the attendant says, handing over the papers, which are all neatly bound in a little jacket. "Have a wonderful flight."

Hadley edges her way toward the windows and surveys the rows of drab gray chairs, most of them occupied and the rest sprouting yellow stuffing at their seams like well-loved teddy bears. She props her backpack on top of her carry-on suitcase and digs for her cell phone, then scrolls through the contacts for her dad's number. He's listed simply as "The Professor," a label she bestowed on him about a year and a half ago, shortly after it was announced that he wouldn't be returning to Connecticut and the word *dad* had become an unpleasant reminder each time she opened her phone.

Her heart quickens now as it begins to ring; though he still calls fairly often, she's probably dialed him only a handful of times. It's nearly midnight there, and when he finally picks up, his voice is thick, slowed by sleep or alcohol or maybe both.

"Hadley?"

"I missed my flight," she says, adopting the clipped tone that comes so naturally when talking to her father these days, a side effect of her general disapproval of him.

"What?"

8

She sighs and repeats herself: "I missed my flight."

In the background, Hadley can hear Charlotte murmuring, and something flares up inside of her, a quick rise of anger. Despite the sugary e-mails the woman has been sending her ever since Dad proposed—filled with wedding plans and photos of their trip to Paris and pleas for Hadley to get involved, all signed with an overzealous "xxoo" (as if one *x* and one *o* weren't sufficient)—it's been exactly one year and ninety-six days since Hadley decided that she hated her, and it will take much more than an invitation to be a bridesmaid to cancel this out.

"Well," Dad says, "did you get another one?"

"Yeah, but it doesn't get in till ten."

"Tomorrow?"

"No, tonight," she says. "I'll be traveling by comet."

Dad ignores this. "That's too late. It's too close to the ceremony. I won't be able to pick you up," he says, and there's a muffled sound as he covers the phone to whisper to Charlotte. "We can probably send Aunt Marilyn to get you."

"Who's Aunt Marilyn?"

"Charlotte's aunt."

"I'm seventeen," Hadley reminds him. "I'm pretty sure I can handle getting a taxi to the church."

"I don't know," Dad says. "It's your first time in London...." He trails off, then clears his throat. "Do you think your mom would be okay with it?"

"Mom's not here," Hadley says. "I guess she caught the first wedding."

There's silence on the other end of the phone.

"It's fine, Dad. I'll meet you at the church tomorrow. Hopefully I won't be too late."

"Okay," he says softly. "I can't wait to see you."

"Yeah," she says, unable to bring herself to say it back to him. "See you tomorrow."

It isn't until after they've hung up that Hadley realizes she didn't even ask how the rehearsal dinner went. She's not all that sure she wants to know.

For a long moment, she just stands there like that, the phone still held tightly in her hand, trying not to think about all that awaits her on the other side of the ocean. The smell of butter from a nearby pretzel stand is making her slightly sick, and she'd like nothing more than to sit down, but the gate is choked with passengers who've spilled over from other areas of the terminal. It's Fourth of July weekend, and the weather maps on the TV screens show a swirling pattern of storms blotting out much of the Midwest. People are staking out their territory, laying claim to sections of the waiting area as if they plan to live there permanently. There are suitcases perched on empty chairs, families camped out around entire corners, greasy McDonald's bags strewn across the floor. As she picks her way over a man sleeping on his backpack, Hadley is keenly aware of the closeness of the ceiling and the press of the walls, the surging presence of the crowd all around her, and she has to remind herself to breathe.

When she spots an empty seat, she hurries in that direction, maneuvering her rolling suitcase through the sea of shoes and trying not to think about just how crushed the silly purple dress will be by the time she arrives tomorrow morning. The plan was to have a few hours to get ready at the hotel before the ceremony, but now she'll have to make a mad dash for the church. Of all her many worries at the moment, this doesn't rank particularly high on Hadley's list, but still, it's a little bit funny to imagine just how horrified Charlotte's friends will be; not having time to get your hair done undoubtedly qualifies as a major catastrophe in their books.

Hadley's pretty sure that *regret* is too slight a word to describe her feelings about agreeing to be a bridesmaid, but she'd been worn down by Charlotte's incessant e-mails and Dad's endless pleas, not to mention Mom's surprising support of the idea.

"I know he's not your favorite person in the world right now," she'd said, "and he's certainly not mine, either. But do you really want to be flipping through that wedding album one day, maybe with your own kids, and wishing you'd been a part of it?"

Hadley really doesn't think she'd mind, actually, but she could see where everyone was going with this, and it had just seemed easier to make them happy, even if it meant enduring the hair spray and the uncomfortable heels and the post-ceremony photo shoot. When the rest of the wedding party—a collection of Charlotte's thirtysomething friends—had learned about the addition of an American teenager, Hadley had been promptly welcomed with a flurry of exclamation points to the e-mail chain that was circulating among the group. And though she'd never met Charlotte before and had spent the last year and a half making sure it stayed that way, she now knew the woman's preferences on a wide range of topics pertaining to the wedding—important issues like strappy sandals vs. closed-toe heels; whether to include baby's breath in the bouquets; and, worst and most scarring of all, lingerie preferences for the bridal shower or, as they called it, the hen party. It was staggering, really, the amount of e-mail a wedding could generate. Hadley knew that some of the women were Charlotte's colleagues at the university art gallery at Oxford, but it was a wonder that any of them had time for jobs of their own. She was scheduled to meet them at the hotel early tomorrow morning, but it now looks as if they'll have to go about zipping their dresses and lining their eyes and curling their hair without her.

Out the window, the sky is a dusky pink now, and the pinpricks of light that outline the planes are beginning to flicker to life. Hadley can make out her reflection in the glass, all blond hair and big eyes, somehow already looking as careworn and rumpled as if the journey were behind her. She wedges herself into a seat between an older man flapping his newspaper so hard she half expects it to up and fly away and a middle-aged woman with an embroidered cat on her turtleneck, knitting away at what could still turn out to be anything.

Three more hours, she thinks, hugging her backpack, then realizes there's no point in counting down the minutes to something you're dreading; it would be far more accurate to say two more days. Two more days and she'll be back home again. Two more days and she can pretend this never happened. Two more days and she'll have survived the weekend she's been dreading for what feels like years.

She readjusts the backpack on her lap, realizing a moment too late that she didn't zip it up all the way, and a few of her things tumble to the floor. Hadley reaches for the lip gloss first, then the gossip magazines, but when she goes to pick up the heavy black book that her father gave her, the boy across the aisle reaches it first.

He glances briefly at the cover before handing it back, and Hadley catches a flicker of recognition in his eyes. It takes her a second to understand that he must think she's the kind of person who reads Dickens in the airport, and she very nearly tells him that she's not; in fact, she's had the book for ages and has never cracked it open. But instead, she smiles in acknowledgment, then turns quite deliberately toward the windows, just in case he might be thinking about striking up a conversation.

Because Hadley doesn't feel like talking right now, not even to someone as cute as he is. She doesn't feel like being here at all, actually. The day ahead of her is like something living and breathing, something that's barreling toward her at an alarming rate, and it seems only a matter of time before it will knock her flat on her back. The dread she feels at the idea of getting on the plane—not to mention getting to London—is something physical; it makes her fidget in her seat, sets her leg bobbing and her fingers twitching.

The man beside her blows his nose loudly, then snaps his newspaper back to attention, and Hadley hopes she's not sitting next to him on her flight. Seven hours is a long time, too big a slice of your day to be left to chance. You would never be expected to take a road trip with someone you didn't know, yet how many times has she flown to Chicago or Denver or Florida beside a complete stranger, elbow to elbow, side by side, as the two of them hurtled across the country together? That's the thing about flying: You could talk to someone for hours and never even know his name, share your deepest secrets and then never see him again.

As the man cranes his neck to read an article his arm brushes against Hadley's, and she stands abruptly, swinging her backpack onto one shoulder. Around her, the gate area is still teeming with people, and she looks longingly toward the windows, wishing she were outside right now. She's not sure she can sit here for three more hours, but the idea of dragging her suitcase through the crowd is daunting. She edges it closer to her empty seat so that it might look reserved, then turns to the lady in the cat turtleneck.

"Would you mind watching my bag for a minute?" she asks, and the woman holds her knitting needles very still and frowns up at her.

"You're not supposed to do that," she says pointedly.

"It's just for a minute or two," Hadley explains, but the woman simply gives her head a little shake, as if she can't bear to be implicated in whatever scenario is about to unfold.

"I can watch it," says the boy across the aisle, and Hadley looks at him—really looks at him—for the first time. His dark hair is a bit too long and there are crumbs down the front of his shirt, but there's something striking about him, too. Maybe it's the accent, which she's pretty sure is British, or the twitch of his mouth as he tries to keep from smiling. But her heart dips unexpectedly when he looks at her, his eyes skipping from Hadley back to the woman, whose lips are set in a thin line of disapproval.

"It's against the *law*," the woman says under her breath, her eyes shifting over to where two bulky security guards are standing just outside the food court.

Hadley glances back at the boy, who offers her a sympathetic smile. "Never mind," she says. "I'll just take it. Thanks anyway."

She begins to gather her things, tucking the book under her arm and swinging her backpack up onto her other shoulder. The woman just barely pulls her feet back as Hadley maneuvers the suitcase past her. When she gets to the end of the waiting area, the colorless carpeting gives way to the linoleum of the corridor, and her suitcase teeters precariously on the rubber ridge that separates the two. It rocks from one wheel to the other, and as Hadley tries to right it the book slips from under her arm. When she stoops to pick it up again, her sweatshirt flutters to the floor as well.

You've got *to be kidding,* Hadley thinks, blowing a strand of hair from her face. But by the time she gathers everything and reaches for her suitcase again, it's somehow no longer there. Spinning around, she's stunned to see the boy standing beside her, his own bag slung over his shoulder. Her eyes travel down to where he's gripping the handle of her suitcase.

"What're you doing?" she asks, blinking at him.

"You looked like you might need some help."

Hadley just stares at him.

"And this way it's perfectly legal," he adds with a grin.

She raises her eyebrows and he straightens up a bit, looking somewhat less sure of himself. It occurs to her that perhaps he's planning to steal her bag, but if that's the case, it's not a very well-planned heist; pretty much the only things in there are a pair of shoes and a dress. And she would be more than happy to lose those.

She stands there for a long moment, wondering what she could have done to have secured herself a porter. But the crowds are surging around them and her backpack is heavy on her shoulders and the boy's eyes are searching hers with something like loneliness, like the very last thing he wants is to be left behind right now. And that's something Hadley can understand, too, and so after a moment she nods in agreement, and he tips the suitcase forward onto its wheels, and they begin to walk.

7:12 PM Eastern Standard Time
12:12 AM Greenwich Mean Time

An announcement comes over the loudspeaker about a passenger missing from his plane, and Hadley can't stop the thought from tiptoeing into her head: What if she were to skip out on her own flight? But as if he can read her mind, the boy in front of her glances back to make sure she's still there, and she realizes she's grateful to have some company on this of all days, unexpected as it may be.

They walk past a row of paneled windows that face out over the tarmac, where the planes are lined up like floats in a parade, and Hadley feels her heart pick up speed at the thought of having to board one soon. Of all the many tight places in the world, the endless nooks and crannies and corners, nothing sets her trembling quite as much as the sight of an airplane.

It was just last year when it happened for the first time, this dizzying worry, a heart-thudding, stomach-churning exercise in panic. In a hotel bathroom in Aspen, with the snow falling fast and thick outside the window and her dad on the phone in the next room, she had the sudden sensation that the walls were too close and getting closer, inching toward her with the steady certainty of a glacier. She stood there trying to measure her breathing, her heart pounding out a rhythm in her ears so loud it nearly drowned out the sound of Dad's muffled voice on the other side of the wall.

"Yeah," he was saying, "and we're supposed to get another six inches tonight, so it should be perfect tomorrow."

They'd been in Aspen for two whole days, doing their best to pretend this spring break was no different from any other. They rose early each morning to get up the mountain before the slopes were too crowded, sat silently with their mugs of hot chocolate in the lodge afterward, played board games at night in front of the fireplace. But the truth was, they spent so much time *not* talking about Mom's absence that it had become the only thing either of them could think about.

Besides, Hadley wasn't stupid. You didn't just pack off to Oxford for a semester, spend your days teaching poetry classes, and then suddenly decide you wanted a divorce without a good reason. And though Mom hadn't said a word about it—had, in fact, grown nearly silent on the subject of Dad in general—Hadley knew that reason must be another woman.

She'd planned to confront him about it on the ski trip, to step off the plane and thrust an accusing finger at him and demand to know why he wasn't coming home. But when she made her way down to the baggage claim to find him waiting for her he looked completely different, with a reddish beard that didn't match his dark hair and a smile so big she could see the caps on his teeth. It had been only six months, but in that time he'd become a near stranger, and it wasn't until he stooped to hug her that he came back again, smelling like cigarette smoke and aftershave, his voice gravelly in her ear as he told her how much he'd missed her. And for some reason, that was even worse. In the end, it's not the changes that will break your heart; it's that tug of familiarity.

And so she'd chickened out, instead spending those first two days watching and waiting, trying to read the lines of his face like a map, searching for clues to explain why their little family had so abruptly fallen apart. When he'd gone off to England the previous fall, they'd all been thrilled. Until then he'd been a professor at a small mid-tier college in Connecticut, so the idea of a fellowship at Oxford—which boasted one of the best literature departments in the world—had been irresistible. But Hadley had been just about to start her sophomore year, and Mom couldn't leave her little wallpaper shop for four whole months, so it was decided that they'd stay behind until Christmas, when they'd join him in England for a couple of weeks of sight-seeing, and then they'd all return home together.

That, of course, never happened.

At the time, Mom had simply announced that there was a change of plans, that they'd be spending Christmas at Hadley's grandparents' house in Maine instead. Hadley half believed her dad would be there to surprise her when they arrived, but on Christmas Eve, it was only Grandma and Pops and enough presents to confirm that everyone was trying to make up for the absence of something else.

For days before that, Hadley had been overhearing her parents' tension-filled phone calls and listening to the sound of her mother crying through the vents of their old house, but it wasn't until the drive home from Maine that Mom finally announced that she and Dad would be split-ting up, and that he'd be staying on for another semester at Oxford.

"It'll just be a separation at first," she said, sliding her eyes from the road over to where Hadley sat numbly, absorb-ing the news one incremental thought at a time—first, *Mom and Dad are getting divorced*, and then, *Dad isn't coming back*.

"There's a whole ocean between you," she said quietly. "How much more separated can you get?"

"Legally," Mom said with a sigh. "We're going to *legally* separate."

"Don't you need to see each other first? Before deciding something like that?"

"Oh, honey," Mom said, taking a hand off the wheel to give Hadley's knee a little pat. "I think it's already been decided."

And so, just two months later, Hadley stood in the bathroom of their Aspen hotel, her toothbrush in hand, as her dad's voice drifted in from the next room. A moment earlier she'd been sure it was Mom calling to check in, and her heart had lifted at the thought. But then she heard him say a name—*Charlotte*—before lowering his voice again.

"No, it's fine," he said. "She's just in the loo."

Hadley felt suddenly cold all over, wondering when her father had become the kind of man to call the bathroom a "loo," to whisper to foreign women on hotel phones, to take his daughter on a ski trip as if it meant something, as if it were a promise, and then return to his new life like it had never even happened.

She took a step closer to the door, her bare feet cold on the tiles.

"I know," he was saying now, his voice soft. "I miss you, too, honey."

Of course, Hadley thought, closing her eyes. *Of course.*

It didn't help that she was right; when had that ever made anything better? She felt a tiny seed of resentment take root inside of her. It was like the pit of a peach, something small and hard and mean, a bitterness she was certain would never dissolve.

She stepped back from the door, feeling her throat go tight and her rib cage swell. In the mirror, she watched the color rise up into her cheeks, and her eyes felt blurred by the heat of the small room. She wrapped her fingers around the edge of the sink, watching her knuckles go white, forcing herself to wait until he was off the phone.

"What's wrong?" Dad asked when she finally emerged from the bathroom, walked straight past him without a word, and then flopped onto one of the beds. "Are you feeling okay?"

"Fine," Hadley said shortly.

But it happened again the next day.

As they rode the elevator down to the lobby the following morning, already warm beneath layers of ski gear, there was a sharp jolt, and then they came to an abrupt stop. They were the only two people in there, and they exchanged a blank look before Dad shrugged and reached for the emergency call button. "Stupid bloody elevator."

Hadley glared at him. "Don't you mean stupid bloody lift?"

"What?"

"Nothing," she muttered, then jabbed at the buttons randomly, lighting up one after another as a rising sense of panic welled up inside of her.

"I don't think that's gonna do anything...." Dad began to say, but he stopped when he seemed to notice something was wrong. "Are you okay?"

Hadley tugged at the collar of her ski jacket, then unzipped it. "No," she said, her heart thumping wildly. "Yes. I don't know. I want to get out of here."

"They'll be here soon," he said. "There's nothing we can do till—"

"No, *now*, Dad," she said, feeling slightly frantic. It was the first time she'd called him Dad since they'd gotten to Aspen; until that point, she'd pretty much avoided calling him anything at all.

His eyes skipped around the tiny elevator. "Are you having a panic attack?" he asked, looking a bit panicky himself. "Has this happened before? Does your mom—"

Hadley shook her head. She wasn't sure what was happening; all she knew was that she needed to get out of there *right now.*

"Hey," Dad said, taking her by the shoulders and forcing her to meet his eyes. "They'll be here in a minute, okay? Just look at me. Don't think about where we are."

"Okay," she muttered, gritting her teeth.

"Okay," he said. "Think about someplace else. Somewhere with open spaces."

She tried to still her frenzied mind, to bring forth some soothing memory, but her brain refused to cooperate. Her face was prickly with heat, and it was hard to focus.

"Pretend you're at the beach," he said. "Or the sky! Imagine the sky, okay? Think about how big it is, how you can't see the end of it."

Hadley screwed her eyes shut and forced herself to picture it, the vast and endless blue marred only by the occasional cloud. The deepness of it, the sheer scope of it, so big it was impossible to know where it ended. She felt her heart begin to slow and her breathing grow even, and she unclenched her sweaty fists. When she opened her eyes again, Dad's face was level with hers, his eyes wide with worry. They stared at each other for what felt like forever, and Hadley realized it was the first time she'd allowed herself to look him in the eye since they'd arrived.

After a moment, the elevator shuddered into motion, and she let out a breath. They rode down the rest of the way in silence, both of them shaken, both of them eager to step outside and stand beneath the enormous stretch of western sky.

Now, in the middle of the crowded terminal, Hadley pulls her eyes away from the windows, from the planes fanned out across the runways like windup toys. Her stomach tightens again; the only time it doesn't help to imagine the sky is when you're thirty thousand feet in the air with nowhere to go but down.

She turns to see that the boy is waiting for her, his hand still wrapped around the handle of her suitcase. He smiles when she catches up, then swings out into the busy corridor, and Hadley hurries to keep up with his long stride. She's concentrating so hard on following his blue shirt that when he stops, she very nearly runs into him. He's taller than she is by at least six inches, and he has to duck his head to speak to her.

"I didn't even ask where you're going."

"London," she says, and he laughs.

"No, I meant *now*. Where are you going now?"

"Oh," she says, rubbing her forehead. "I don't know, actually. To get dinner, maybe? I just didn't want to sit there forever."

This is not entirely true; she'd been heading to the bathroom, but she can't quite bring herself to tell him this. The thought of him waiting politely just outside while she stands in line for the toilet is more than she can bear.

"Okay," he says, looking down at her, his dark hair falling across his forehead. When he smiles, she notices that he has a dimple on only one side, and there's something about this that makes him seem endearingly off-balance. "Where to, then?"

Hadley stands on her tiptoes, turning in a small circle to get a sense of the restaurant choices, a bleak collection of pizza and burger stands. She isn't sure whether he'll be joining her, and this possibility gives the decision a slightly frenzied feel; she can practically feel him waiting beside her, and her whole body is tense as she tries to think of the option that's the least likely to leave her with food all over her face, just in case he decides to come along.

After what seems like forever, she points to a deli just a few gates down, and he heads off in that direction obligingly, her red suitcase in tow. When they get there, he readjusts the bag on his shoulder and squints up at the menu.

"This is a good idea," he says. "The plane food'll be rubbish."

"Where are you headed?" Hadley asks as they join the line.

"London as well."

"Really? What seat?"

He reaches into the back pocket of his jeans and produces his ticket, bent in half and ripped at one corner. "Eighteen-C."

"I'm eighteen-A," she tells him, and he smiles.

"Just missed."

She nods at his garment bag, which is still resting on his shoulder, his finger hooked around the hanger. "You going over for a wedding, too?"

He hesitates, then jerks his chin up in the first half of a nod.

"So am I," she says. "Wouldn't it be weird if it was the same one?"

"Not likely," he says, giving her an odd look, and she immediately feels silly. Of course it's not the same one. She hopes he doesn't think she's under the impression that London is some kind of backwater town where everyone knows everyone else. Hadley's never been out of the country before, but she knows enough to know that London is enormous; it is, in her limited experience, a big enough place to lose someone entirely.

The boy looks as if he's about to say something more, then turns and gestures toward the menu instead. "Do you know what you'd like?"

Do I know what I'd like? Hadley thinks.

She'd like to go home.

She'd like for home to be the way it once was.

She'd like to be going anywhere but her father's wedding.

She'd like to *be* anywhere but this airport.

She'd like to know his name.

After a moment, she looks up at him.

"Not yet," she says. "I'm still deciding."

3

Despite having ordered her turkey sandwich without mayo, Hadley can see the white goo oozing onto the crust as she carries her food to an empty table, and her stomach lurches at the sight. She's debating whether it would be better to suffer through eating it or risk looking like an idiot as she scrapes it off, and eventually settles for looking like an idiot, ignoring the boy's raised eyebrows as she dissects her dinner with all the care of a biology experiment. She wrinkles her nose as she sets aside the lettuce and tomato, ridding each disassembled piece of the clinging white globs.

"That's some nice work there," he says around a mouthful of roast beef, and Hadley nods matter-of-factly.

"I have a fear of mayo, so I've actually gotten pretty good at this over the years."

"You have a fear of *mayo?*"

She nods again. "It's in my top three or four."

"What are the others?" he asks with a grin. "I mean, what could *possibly* be worse than mayonnaise?"

"Dentists," she offers. "Spiders. Ovens."

"Ovens? So I take it you're not much of a cook."

"And small spaces," she says, a bit more quietly.

He tilts his head to one side. "So what do you do on the plane?"

Hadley shrugs. "Grit my teeth and hope for the best."

"Not a bad tactic," he says with a laugh. "Does it work?"

She doesn't answer, struck by a small flash of alarm. It's almost worse when she forgets about it for a moment, because it never fails to come rushing back again with renewed force, like some sort of demented boomerang.

"Well," says the boy, propping his elbows on the table, "claustrophobia is nothing compared to mayo-phobia, and look how well you're conquering that." He nods at the plastic knife in her hand, which is caked with mayonnaise and bread crumbs. Hadley smiles at him gratefully.

As they eat, their eyes drift to the television set in the corner of the café, where the weather updates are flashed over and over again. Hadley tries to focus on her dinner, but she can't help sneaking a sideways glance at him every now and then, and each time, her stomach does a little jig entirely unrelated to the traces of mayo still left in her sandwich.

She's only ever had one boyfriend, Mitchell Kelly: athletic, uncomplicated, and endlessly dull. They'd dated for much of last year—their junior year—and though she'd loved watching him on the soccer field (the way he'd wave to her on the sidelines), and though she was always happy to see him in the halls at school (the way he'd lift her off her feet when he hugged her), and though she'd cried to each and every one of her friends when he broke up with her just four short months ago, their brief relationship now strikes her as the most obvious mistake in the world.

It seems impossible that she could have liked someone like Mitchell when there was someone like this guy in the world, someone tall and lanky, with tousled hair and startling green eyes and a speck of mustard on his chin, like the one small imperfection that makes the whole painting work somehow.

Is it possible not to ever know your type—not to even know you *have* a type—until quite suddenly you do?

Hadley twists her napkin underneath the table. It occurs to her that she's been referring to him in her head simply as "The Brit," and so she finally leans across the table, scattering the crumbs from their sandwiches, and asks his name.

"Right," he says, blinking at her. "I guess that part *does* traditionally come first. I'm Oliver."

"As in Twist?"

"Wow," he says with a grin. "And they say Americans are uncultured."

She narrows her eyes at him in mock anger. "Funny."

"And you?"

"Hadley."

"Hadley," he repeats with a nod. "That's pretty."

She knows he's only talking about her name, but she's still unaccountably flattered. Maybe it's the accent, or the way he's looking at her with such interest right now, but there's something about him that makes her heart quicken in the way it does when she's surprised. And she supposes that might just be it: the surprise of it all. She's spent so much energy dreading this trip that she hadn't been prepared for the possibility that something good might come out of it, too, something unexpected.

"You don't want your pickle?" he asks, leaning forward, and Hadley shakes her head and pushes her plate across the table to him. He eats it in two bites, then sits back again. "Ever been to London before?"

"Never," she says, a bit too forcefully.

He laughs. "It's not *that* bad."

"No, I'm sure it's not," she says, biting her lip. "Do you live there?"

"I grew up there."

"So where do you live now?"

"Connecticut, I guess," he says. "I go to Yale."

Hadley's unable to hide her surprise. "You do?"

"What, I don't look like a proper Yalie to you?"

"No, it's just so *close*."

"To what?"

She hadn't meant to say that, and now she feels her

cheeks go warm. "To where I live," she says, then rushes on. "It's just that with your accent, I figured you—"

"Were a London street urchin?"

Hadley shakes her head quickly, completely embarrassed now, but he's laughing.

"I'm only playing," he says. "I just finished up my first year there."

"So how come you're not home for the summer?"

"I like it over here," he says with a shrug. "Plus I won a summer research grant, so I'm sort of required to stick around."

"What kind of research?"

"I'm studying the fermentation process of mayonnaise."

"You are not," she says, laughing, and Oliver frowns.

"I am," he says. "It's very important work. Did you know that twenty-four percent of all mayonnaise is actually laced with vanilla ice cream?"

"That *does* sound important," she says. "But what are you really studying?"

A man bumps hard into the back of Hadley's chair as he walks past, then moves on without apologizing, and Oliver grins. "Patterns of congestion in U.S. airports."

"You're ridiculous," Hadley says, shaking her head. She looks off toward the busy corridor. "But if you could do something about these crowds, I wouldn't mind it. I hate airports."

"Really?" Oliver says. "I love them."

She's convinced, for a moment, that he's still teasing her, but then realizes he's serious.

"I like how you're neither here nor there. And how there's nowhere else you're meant to be while waiting. You're just sort of . . . suspended."

"That's fine, I guess," she says, playing with the tab on her soda can, "if it weren't for the crowds."

He glances over his shoulder. "They're not always as bad as this."

"They are if you're me." She looks over at the screens displaying arrivals and departures, many of the green letters blinking to indicate delays or cancellations.

"We've still got some time," Oliver says, and Hadley sighs.

"I know, but I missed my flight earlier, so this sort of feels like a stay of execution."

"You were supposed to be on the last one?"

She nods.

"What time's the wedding?"

"Noon," she says, and he makes a face.

"That'll be tough to make."

"So I've heard," she says. "What time's yours?"

He lowers his eyes. "I'm meant to be at the church at two."

"So you'll be fine."

"Yeah," he says. "I suppose I will."

They sit in silence, each looking at the table, until the muffled sound of a phone ringing comes from Oliver's pocket. He fishes it out, staring at it with a look of great intensity while it carries on, until at last he seems to come to a decision and stands abruptly.

"I should really take this," he tells her, sidestepping away from the table. "Sorry."

Hadley waves a hand. "It's okay," she says. "Go."

She watches as he walks away, picking a path across the crowded concourse, the phone at his ear. His head is ducked, and there's something hunched about him, the curve of his shoulders, the bend of his neck, that makes him seem different now, a less substantial version of the Oliver she's been talking to, and she wonders who might be on the other end of the call. It occurs to her that it could very well be a girlfriend, some beautiful and brilliant student from Yale who wears trendy glasses and a peacoat and would never be so disorganized as to miss a flight by four minutes.

Hadley's surprised by how quickly she pushes the thought away.

She glances down at her own phone, realizing she should probably call her mother and let her know about the change in flights. But her stomach flutters at the thought of how they parted earlier, the ride to the airport in stony silence and then Hadley's unforgiving speech in the departures lane. She knows she has a tendency to shoot her mouth off—Dad always used to joke that she was born without a filter—but who could expect her to be completely rational on the day she's been dreading for months?

She woke up this morning feeling tense all over; her neck and shoulders were sore, and there was a dull throbbing at the back of her head. It wasn't just the wedding, or the fact that she'd soon be forced to meet Charlotte, who she'd spent so much energy pretending didn't exist; it was that this weekend would mark the official end of their family.

Hadley knows this isn't some Disney movie. Her parents aren't ever getting back together. The truth is, she doesn't even really *want* them to anymore. Dad's obviously happy, and for the most part Mom seems to be, too; she's been dating their town dentist, Harrison Doyle, for more than a year now. But even so, this wedding will put a period at the end of a sentence that wasn't supposed to have ended yet, and Hadley isn't sure she's ready to watch as that happens.

In the end, though, she hadn't really had a choice.

"He's still your father," Mom kept telling her. "He's obviously not perfect, but it's important to him that you be there. It's just one day, you know? He's not asking for much."

But it seemed to Hadley that he *was*, that all he did was ask: for her forgiveness, for more time together, for her to give Charlotte a chance. He asked and he asked and he asked, and he never gave a thing. She wanted to take her mother by the shoulders and shake some sense into her. He'd broken their trust, he'd broken Mom's heart, he'd broken their family. And now he was just going to marry this woman, as if none of that mattered. As if it were far easier to start over completely than to try to put everything back together again.

Mom always insisted they were better off this way. All three of them. "I know it's hard to believe," she'd say, maddeningly levelheaded about the whole thing, "but it was for the best. It really was. You'll understand when you're older."

But Hadley's pretty sure she understands already, and

she suspects the problem is that it just hasn't fully sunk in for Mom yet. There's always a gap between the burn and the sting of it, the pain and the realization. For those first few weeks after Christmas, Hadley would lie awake at night and listen to the sound of her mother crying; for a few days, Mom would refuse to speak of Dad at all, and then she'd talk of nothing else the next, back and forth like a seesaw until one day, about six weeks later, she snapped back, suddenly and without fanfare, radiating a calm acceptance that mystifies Hadley even now.

But the scars were there, too. Harrison had asked Mom to marry him three times now, each time in an increasingly creative fashion—a romantic picnic, a ring in her champagne, and then, finally, a string quartet in the park—but she'd said no again and again and again, and Hadley is certain it's because she still hasn't recovered from what happened with Dad. You can't survive a rift that big without it leaving a mark.

And so this morning, just a plane ride away from seeing the source of all their problems, Hadley woke up in a rotten mood. If everything had gone smoothly, this might have translated into a few sarcastic comments and the occasional grumble on the ride to the airport. But there was a message from Charlotte first thing, reminding her what time to be at the hotel to get ready, and the sound of her clipped British accent set Hadley's teeth on edge in a way that meant the rest of the day was as good as doomed.

Later, of course, her suitcase refused to zip, and Mom

nixed the chandelier earrings she'd planned to wear for the ceremony, then proceeded to ask her eighty-five times whether she had her passport. The toast was burned and Hadley got jam on her sweatshirt and when she drove the car to the drugstore to pick up a mini bottle of shampoo, it began to rain and one of the windshield wipers broke and she ended up waiting at the gas station for nearly forty-five minutes behind a guy who didn't know how to check his own oil. And all the while, the clock kept lurching forward toward the time when they'd have to leave. So when she walked back into the house and threw the keys on the kitchen table, she was in no mood for Mom's eighty-sixth inquiry about her passport.

"Yes," she snapped. "I *have* it."

"I'm just asking," Mom said, raising her eyebrows innocently, and Hadley gave her a mutinous look.

"Sure you don't want to march me onto the plane, too?"

"What's that supposed to mean?"

"Or maybe you should escort me all the way to London to make sure I actually go."

There was a note of warning in Mom's voice. "Hadley."

"I mean, why should *I* be the only one who has to watch him get married to that woman? I don't understand why I have to go at all, much less by myself."

Mom pursed her lips in a look that unmistakably conveyed her disappointment, but by then, Hadley didn't really even care.

Later, they rode the entire way to the airport in stubborn silence, an encore performance of the fight they'd been having for weeks now. And by the time they pulled up to the departures area, every part of Hadley seemed to be tingling with a kind of nervous energy.

Mom switched off the engine, but neither of them moved to get out of the car.

"It'll be fine," Mom said after a moment, her voice soft. "It really will."

Hadley swiveled to face her. "He's getting *married,* Mom. How can it be fine?"

"I just think it's important that you be there—"

"Yeah, I know," she said sharply, cutting her off. "You've mentioned that."

"It'll be fine," Mom said again.

Hadley grabbed her sweatshirt and unbuckled her seat belt. "Well, then it's your fault if anything happens."

"Like what?" Mom asked wearily, and Hadley—buzzing with a kind of anger that made her feel both entirely invincible and incredibly young—reached out to fling open the door.

"Like if my plane crashes or something," she said, not really even sure why she was saying it, except that she was bitter and frustrated and scared, and isn't that how most things like that get said? "Then you'll have managed to lose *both* of us."

They stared at each other, the awful, unrecallable words settling between them like so many bricks, and after a moment Hadley stepped out of the car, swinging her backpack up onto her shoulder and then grabbing her suitcase from the backseat.

"Hadley," Mom said, jumping out on the other side and looking at her from across the hood. "Don't just—"

"I'll call you when I get there," Hadley said, already heading toward the terminal. She could feel Mom watching her the whole way, but some fragile instinct, some mistaken sense of pride, made her refuse to turn around again.

Now, sitting in the little airport café, her thumb hovers over the button on her phone. She takes a deep breath before pressing it, her heart pounding in the quiet spaces between rings.

The words she spoke earlier are still echoing in her mind; Hadley isn't superstitious by nature, but that she so thoughtlessly invoked the possibility of a plane crash right before her flight is nearly enough to make her sick. She thinks about the plane she was supposed to take, already well on its way across the ocean by now, and she feels a sharp sting of regret, hoping that she didn't somehow mess with the mysterious workings of timing and chance.

A part of her is relieved when she gets her mom's voice mail. As she starts to leave a message about the change in plans, she sees Oliver approaching again. For a moment she thinks she recognizes something in the look on his face, the same tortured worry she can feel in herself right now, but when he spots her something shifts, and he's back again, looking unruffled and almost cheerful, an easy smile lighting his eyes.

Hadley has trailed off in the middle of her message, and Oliver points to her phone as he grabs his bag, then jerks his thumb in the direction of the gate. She opens her mouth to tell him she'll only be a minute, but he's already off, and so she finishes the message hastily.

"So I'll call when I get there tomorrow," she says into the phone, her voice wavering slightly. "And Mom? I'm sorry about before, okay? I didn't mean it."

Afterward, when she heads back to the gate, she scans the area for Oliver's blue shirt, but he's nowhere in sight. Rather than wait for him amid the crowd of restless travelers, she circles back to use the bathroom, then pokes around the gift shops and bookstores and newspaper stands, wandering the terminal until it's finally time to board.

As she falls into line, Hadley realizes she's almost too tired to even be anxious at this point. It feels like she's been here for days now, and there's so much more ahead of her to worry about, too: the closeness of the cabin, the panicky feeling that comes with no escape route. There's the wedding and the reception, meeting Charlotte, and seeing Dad for the first time in more than a year. But for now, she just wants to put on her headphones, close her eyes, and sleep. To be set in motion, sent careening across the ocean without any effort on her part, seems almost like a miracle.

When it's her turn to hand over her ticket, the flight attendant smiles from beneath his mustache. "Scared of flying?"

Hadley forces herself to unclench her hand, where she's been gripping the handle of her suitcase with white knuckles. She smiles ruefully.

"Scared of landing," she says, then steps onto the plane anyway.

4

9:58 PM Eastern Standard Time
2:58 AM Greenwich Mean Time

By the time Oliver appears at the top of the aisle, Hadley is
already sitting by the window with her seat belt fastened
and her bag stowed safely in the overhead bin. She's spent
the past seven minutes pretending she wasn't interested in
his arrival, counting planes out the window and examining the pattern on the back of the seat in front of her. But
really, she's just been waiting for him, and when he finally
arrives at their row she finds herself blushing for no good
reason other than that he's quite suddenly looming over
her with that tilted grin of his. There's a kind of unfamiliar
electricity that goes through her at the nearness of him,
and she can't help wondering if he feels it, too.

"Lost you in there," he says, and she manages a nod, happy to be found again.

He hefts his hanging bag up above before scooting into the middle seat beside her, awkwardly arranging his too-long legs in front of him and situating the rest of himself between the unforgiving armrests. Hadley glances at him, her heart thudding at his sudden proximity, at the casual way he's positioned himself so close to her.

"I'll just stay for a minute," he says, leaning back. "Till somebody else comes."

She realizes that a part of her is already composing the story for the benefit of her friends: the one about how she met a cute guy with a great accent on a plane and they spent the whole time talking. But the other part of her, the more practical part, is worried about arriving in London tomorrow morning for her father's wedding without having slept. Because how could she possibly go to sleep with him beside her like this? His elbow is brushing against hers and their kneecaps are nearly touching; there's a dizzying smell to him, too, a wonderfully boyish mixture of deodorant and shampoo.

He pulls a few things from his pocket, thumbing through a pile of change until he eventually finds a lint-covered piece of wrapped candy, which he offers her first, then pops into his mouth.

"How old is that thing?" she asks, her nose wrinkled.

"Ancient. I'm pretty sure I dug it out of a sweet bowl the last time I was home."

"Let me guess," she says. "It was part of a study on the effects of sugar over time."

He grins. "Something like that."

"What are you really studying?"

"It's top secret," he tells her, his face utterly serious. "And you seem nice, so I don't want to have to kill you."

"Gee, thanks," she says. "Can you at least tell me your major? Or is that classified, too?"

"Probably psychology," he says. "Though I'm still sorting it out."

"Ah," Hadley says. "So *that* explains all the mind games."

Oliver laughs. "You say mind games, I say research."

"I guess I better watch what I say, then, if I'm being analyzed."

"That's true," he says. "I'm keeping an eye on you."

"And?"

He gives her a sideways smile. "Too soon to tell."

Behind him, an elderly woman pauses at their row, squinting down at her ticket. She's wearing a flowered dress and has white hair so delicate you can see right through to her scalp. Her hand trembles a bit as she points at the number posted above them.

"I think you're in my seat," she says, worrying the edges of her ticket with her thumb, and beside Hadley, Oliver stands up so fast he hits his head on the air-conditioning panel.

"Sorry," he's saying as he attempts to maneuver out of her way, his cramped overtures doing little to fix things in such a tight space. "I was just there for a moment."

The woman looks at him carefully, then her gaze slides over to Hadley, and they can almost see the idea of it dawning on her, the corners of her watery eyes creasing.

"Oh," she says, bringing her hands together with a soft clap. "I didn't realize you were *together.*" She drops her purse on the end seat. "You two stay put. I'll be just fine here."

Oliver looks like he's trying not to laugh, but Hadley's busy worrying about the fact that he just lost his spot, because who wants to spend seven hours stuck in the middle seat? But as the woman lowers herself gingerly into the rough fabric of her seat, he smiles back at Hadley reassuringly, and she can't help feeling a bit relieved. Because the truth is that now that he's here, she can't imagine it any other way. Now that he's here, she worries that crossing an entire ocean with someone between them might be something like torture.

"So," the woman asks, digging through her purse and emerging with a pair of foam earplugs, "how did you two meet?"

They exchange a quick glance.

"Believe it or not," Oliver says, "it was in an airport."

"How wonderful!" she exclaims, looking positively delighted. "And how did it happen?"

"Well," he begins, sitting up a bit taller, "I was being quite gallant, actually, and offered to help with her suitcase. And then we started talking, and one thing led to another...."

46

Hadley grins. "And he's been carrying my suitcase ever since."

"It's what any true gentleman would do," Oliver says with exaggerated modesty.

"Especially the really gallant ones."

The old woman seems pleased by this, her face folding into a map of tiny wrinkles. "And here you both are."

Oliver smiles. "Here we are."

Hadley's surprised by the force of the wish that wells up inside of her just then: She wishes that it were true, all of it. That it were more than just a story. That it were *their* story.

But then he turns to face her again and the spell is broken. His eyes are practically shining with amusement as he checks to be sure she's still sharing in the joke. Hadley manages a small smile before he swivels back to the woman, who has launched into a story about how she met her husband.

Things like this don't just happen, Hadley thinks. Not really. Not to her.

"...and our youngest is forty-two," the old woman is saying to Oliver. The skin of her neck hangs down in loose folds that quiver like Jell-O when she speaks, and Hadley brings a hand to her own neck reflexively, running her thumb and forefinger along her throat. "And in August it will be fifty-two years together."

"Wow," Oliver says. "That's amazing."

"I wouldn't call it amazing," the woman says, blinking. "It's easy when you find the right person."

The aisle is now clear except for the flight attendants,

who are marching up and down on seat-belt patrol, and the woman pulls a water bottle out of her purse, then opens her wrinkled palm to reveal a sleeping pill.

"When you're on the other side of it," she says, "fifty-two years can seem like about fifty-two minutes." She tips her head back and swallows the pill. "Just like when you're *young* and in love, a seven-hour plane ride can seem like a lifetime."

Oliver pats his knees, which are shoved up against the seat in front of him. "Hope not," he jokes, but the woman only smiles.

"I have no doubt," she says, stuffing a yellow earplug into one ear, and then repeating the gesture on the other side. "Enjoy the flight."

"You, too," Hadley says, but the woman's head has already fallen to one side, and just like that, she begins to snore.

Beneath their feet, the plane vibrates as the engines rumble to life. One of the flight attendants reminds them over the speaker that there will be no smoking, and that everyone should stay seated until the captain has turned off the FASTEN SEAT BELT sign. Another demonstrates the safe use of flotation devices and air masks, her words like a chant, empty and automatic, as the vast majority of the passengers set about ignoring her, examining their newspapers or magazines, shutting off their cell phones and opening their books.

Hadley grabs the laminated safety instructions from the seat pocket in front of her and frowns at the cartoon men and women who seem weirdly delighted to be bailing out of a series of cartoon planes. Beside her, Oliver stifles a laugh, and she glances up again.

"What?"

"I've just never seen anyone actually read one of those things before."

"Well," she says, "then you're very lucky to be sitting next to me."

"Just in general?"

She grins. "Well, particularly in case of an emergency."

"Right," he says. "I feel incredibly safe. When I'm knocked unconscious by my tray table during some sort of emergency landing, I can't wait to see all five-foot-nothing of you carry me out of here."

Hadley's face falls. "Don't even joke about it."

"Sorry," he says, inching closer. He places a hand on her knee, an act so unconscious that he doesn't seem to realize what he's done until Hadley glances down in surprise at his palm, warm against her bare leg. He draws back abruptly, looking a bit stunned himself, then shakes his head. "The flight'll be fine. I didn't mean it."

"It's okay," she says quietly. "I'm not usually quite so superstitious."

Out the window, a few men in neon yellow vests are circling the enormous plane, and Hadley leans over to watch. The old woman on the aisle coughs in her sleep, and they both turn back around, but she's resting peacefully again, her eyelids fluttering.

"Fifty-two years," Oliver says, letting out a low whistle. "That's impressive."

"I'm not sure I even believe in marriage," Hadley says, and he looks surprised.

"Aren't you on your way to a wedding?"

"Yeah," she says with a nod. "But that's what I mean."

He looks at her blankly.

"It shouldn't be this big fuss, where you drag everyone halfway across the world to witness your love. If you want to share your life together, fine. But it's between two people, and that should be enough. Why the big show? Why rub it in everyone's faces?"

Oliver runs a hand along his jaw, obviously not quite sure what to think. "It sounds like it's weddings you don't believe in," he says finally. "Not marriage."

"I'm not such a big fan of either at the moment."

"I don't know," he says. "I think they're kind of nice."

"They're not," she insists. "They're all for show. You shouldn't need to prove anything if you really mean it. It should be a whole lot simpler than that. It should mean something."

"I think it does," Oliver says quietly. "It's a promise."

"I guess so," she says, unable to keep the sigh out of her voice. "But not everyone keeps that promise." She looks over toward the woman, still fast asleep. "Not everyone makes it fifty-two years, and if you do, it doesn't matter that you once stood in front of all those people and said that you would. The important part is that you had someone to stick by you all that time. Even when everything sucked."

He laughs. "Marriage: for when everything sucks."

"Seriously," Hadley insists. "How else do you know that it means something? Unless someone's there to hold your hand during the bad times?"

"So that's it?" Oliver says. "No wedding, no marriage, just someone there to hold your hand when things are rough?"

"That's it," she says with a nod.

Oliver shakes his head in wonder. "Whose wedding *is* this? An ex-boyfriend of yours?"

Hadley can't help the laughter that escapes her.

"What?"

"My ex-boyfriend spends most of his time playing video games, and the rest delivering pizzas. It's just funny to imagine him as a groom."

"I thought you might be a bit young to be a woman scorned."

"I'm seventeen," she says indignantly, and he holds up his hands in surrender.

The plane begins to push back from the gate, and Oliver leans closer to peer out the window. There are lights stretched out as far as they can see, like reflections of the stars, making great constellations of the runways, where dozens of planes sit waiting their turn. Hadley's hands are braided together in her lap, and she takes a deep breath.

"So," Oliver says, sitting back again. "I guess we jumped right into the deep end, huh?"

"What do you mean?"

"Just that a discussion about the definition of true love is usually something you talk about after three months, not three hours."

"According to her," Hadley says, jutting her chin to Oliver's right, "three hours is more like three years."

"Yes, well, that's if you're in love."

"Right. So, not us."

"No," Oliver agrees with a grin. "Not us. An hour's an hour. And we're doing this all wrong."

"How do you figure?"

"I know your feelings on matrimony, but we haven't even covered the really important stuff yet, like your favorite color or your favorite food."

"Blue and Mexican."

He nods appraisingly. "That's respectable. For me, green and curry."

"Curry?" She makes a face. "Really?"

"Hey," he says. "No judging. What else?"

The lights in the cabin are dimmed for takeoff as the engine revs up below them, and Hadley closes her eyes, just for a moment. "What else what?"

"Favorite animal?"

"I don't know," she says, opening her eyes again. "Dogs?"

Oliver shakes his head. "Too boring. Try again."

"Elephants, then."

"Really?"

Hadley nods.

"How come?"

"As a kid, I couldn't sleep without this ratty stuffed elephant," she explains, not sure what made her think of it now. Maybe it's that she'll soon be seeing her dad again, or maybe it's just the plane keying up beneath her, prompting a childish wish for her old security blanket.

"I'm not sure that counts."

"Clearly you never met Elephant."

He laughs. "Did you come up with that name all by yourself?"

"Damn right," she says, smiling at the thought. He'd had glassy black eyes and soft floppy ears and braided strings for a tail, and he always managed to make everything better. From having to eat vegetables or wear itchy tights to stubbing her toe or being stuck in bed with a sore throat, Elephant was the antidote to it all. Over time, he'd lost one eye and most of his tail; he'd been cried on and sneezed on and sat on, but still, whenever Hadley was upset about something, Dad would simply rest a hand on top of her head and steer her upstairs.

"Time to consult the elephant," he'd announce, and somehow, it always worked. It's really only now that it occurs to her that Dad probably deserved more of the credit than the little elephant.

Oliver is looking at her with amusement. "I'm still not convinced it counts."

"Fine," Hadley says. "What's *your* favorite animal?"

"The American eagle."

She laughs. "I don't believe you."

"Me?" he asks, bringing a hand to his heart. "Is it wrong to love an animal that also happens to be a symbol of freedom?"

"Now you're just making fun of me."

"Maybe a little," he says with a grin. "But is it working?"

"What, me getting closer to muzzling you?"

"No," he says quietly. "Me distracting you."

"From what?"

"Your claustrophobia."

She smiles at him gratefully. "A little," she says. "Though it's not as bad until we get up in the air."

"How come?" he asks. "Plenty of wide open spaces up there."

"But no escape route."

"Ah," he says. "So you're looking for an escape route."

Hadley nods. "Always."

"Figures," he says, sighing dramatically. "I get that from girls a lot."

She lets out a short laugh, then closes her eyes again when the plane begins to pick up speed, barreling down the runway with a rush of noise. They're tipped back in their seats as momentum gives way to gravity, the plane tilting backward until—with a final bounce of the wheels—they're set aloft like a giant metal bird.

Hadley wraps a hand around the armrest as they climb higher into the night sky, the lights below fading into pixelated grids. Her ears begin to pop as the pressure builds, and she presses her forehead against the window, dreading the moment when they'll push through the low-hanging bank of clouds and the ground will disappear beneath them, when they'll be surrounded by nothing but the vast and endless sky.

Out the window, the outlines of parking lots and housing developments are growing distant as everything starts to blend together. Hadley watches the world shift and blur into new shapes, the streetlamps with their yellow-orange glow, the long ribbons of highway. She sits up straighter, her forehead cool against the Plexiglas as she strains to keep sight of it all. What she fears isn't flying so much as being set adrift. But for now, they're still low enough to see the lit windows of the buildings below. For now, Oliver is beside her, keeping the clouds at bay.

5

10:36 PM Eastern Standard Time
3:36 AM Greenwich Mean Time

They've been in the air only a few minutes when Oliver seems to decide it's safe to speak to her again. At the sound of his voice near her ear, Hadley feels something inside of her loosening, and she unclenches her hands one finger at a time.

"Once," he says, "I was flying to California on the Fourth of July."

She turns her head, just slightly.

"It was a clear night, and you could see all the little fireworks displays along the way, these tiny flares going off below, one town after another."

Hadley leans to the window again, her heart pounding as she stares at the emptiness below, the sheer nothingness of it all. She closes her eyes and tries to imagine fireworks instead.

"If you didn't know what they were, it probably would've looked terrifying, but from up above they were sort of pretty, just really silent and small. It was hard to imagine they were the same huge explosions you see from the ground." He pauses for a moment. "I suppose it's all a matter of perspective."

She twists toward him again, searching his face. "Is that supposed to help?" she asks, though not unkindly. She's simply trying to find the lesson in the story.

"No, not really," he says with a sheepish grin. "I was just trying to distract you again."

She smiles. "Thanks. Got anything else?"

"Loads," he says. "I could talk your ear off."

"For seven hours?"

"I'm up for the challenge," he tells her.

The plane has leveled out now, and when she starts to feel dizzy, Hadley tries to focus on the seat in front of her, which is occupied by a man with large ears and thinning hair at the crown of his head; not so much that he could be called bald, exactly, but just enough to give a suggestion of the baldness to come. It's like reading a map of the future, and she wonders if there are such telltale signs on everyone, hidden clues to the people they'll one day become. Had anyone guessed, for example, that the lady on the aisle would eventually cease to look at the world through brilliant blue eyes, and instead see everything from behind a filmy haze? Or that the man sitting kitty-corner to them would have to hold one hand with the other to keep it still?

What she's really thinking about, though, is her father.

What she's really wondering is whether *he's* changed.

The air in the plane is dry and stale, rough against the inside of her nose, and Hadley closes her sore eyes and holds her breath for a moment as if she were underwater, something not difficult to imagine as they swim through the borderless night sky. She blinks her eyes open and reaches out abruptly, pulling down the plastic window shade. Oliver glances at her with raised eyebrows but says nothing.

A memory arrives, swift and unwelcome, of a flight with her father, years ago, though it's hard now to be certain how many. She remembers how he absently fiddled with the window shade, dropping it shut and then thrusting it open again, over and over, up and then down, until the passengers across the aisle had leaned forward with their eyebrows knit and their mouths pursed. When the seatbelt sign had finally blinked off, he'd lurched up from his seat, bending to give Hadley a kiss on the forehead as he scooted past her and out into the aisle. For two hours he'd paced the narrow path from first class all the way back to the bathrooms, stopping now and then to lean over and ask what Hadley was doing, *how* she was doing, what she was reading, and then he'd be off again, looking like someone impatiently waiting for his bus to arrive.

Had he always been so restless? It was hard to know for sure.

Now she turns to Oliver. "So, has your dad come over to visit you much?" she asks, and he looks at her with slightly startled eyes. She stares back at him, equally surprised by her question. What she'd meant to say was *your parents*. Have *your parents* come over to visit much? The word *dad* had slipped out nearly unconsciously.

Oliver clears his throat and drops his hands to his lap, where he twists the extra fabric of his seat belt into a tight bundle. "Just my mum, actually," he says. "She brought me out at the start of the year. Couldn't bear to send me off to school in America without making my bed first."

"That's cute," Hadley says, trying not to think of her own mother, of the fight they had earlier. "She sounds sweet."

She waits for Oliver to say more, or perhaps to ask about *her* family, because it seems like the natural progression of conversation for two people with nowhere to go and hours to spare. But all he does is silently trace a finger over the letters stitched into the seat in front of them: FASTEN SEAT BELT WHILE SEATED.

Above them, one of the blackened television screens brightens, and there's an announcement about the in-flight movie. It's an animated film about a family of ducks, one that Hadley's actually seen, and when Oliver groans, she's about to deny the whole thing. But then she twists in her seat and eyes him critically.

"There's nothing wrong with ducks," she tells him, and he rolls his eyes.

"*Talking* ducks?"

Hadley grins. "They sing, too."

"Don't tell me," he says. "You've already seen it."

She holds up two fingers. "Twice."

"You *do* know that it's meant for five-year-olds, right?"

"Five- to *eight*-year-olds, thank you very much."

"And how old are you again?"

"Old enough to appreciate our web-footed friends."

"You," he says, laughing in spite of himself, "are mad as a hatter."

"Wait a second," Hadley says, looking at him with mock horror. "Is that a reference to a . . . *cartoon*?"

"No, genius. It's a reference to a famous work of literature by Lewis Carroll. But once again, I can see how well that American education is working for you."

"Hey," she says, giving him a light whack on the chest, a gesture so natural she doesn't even pause to think it over until it's too late. He smiles at her, clearly amused. "Last time I checked, you'd chosen an American college."

"True," he says. "But I'm able to supplement it with my wealth of British intelligence and charm."

"Right," Hadley says. "Charm. When do I get to see some of *that*?"

He twists his mouth up at the corners. "Didn't some guy help carry your suitcase earlier?"

"Oh, yeah," she says, tapping a finger against her chin. "*That* guy. He was great. I wonder where he went?"

"That's what I'm studying, actually," he says with a grin. "This summer."

"What?"

"Split personality disorder in eighteen-year-old males."

"Of course," she says. "The one thing more frightening than mayo."

To her surprise, a fly appears near her ear, and Hadley tries unsuccessfully to swipe it away. A moment later it's buzzing nearby again, making infuriating loops around their heads like a relentless figure skater.

"I wonder if he bought a ticket," Oliver says.

"Probably just a stowaway."

"Poor bloke has no idea he's going to end up in another country altogether."

"Yeah, where everyone talks funny."

Oliver waves a hand to shoo the fly away.

"Do you think he thinks he's flying really fast?" Hadley asks. "Like when you walk on one of those conveyor belt things? He's probably pretty psyched to be making such good time."

"Haven't you ever taken physics?" Oliver asks, rolling his eyes. "It's relativity. He's flying with respect to the plane, not with respect to the ground."

"Okay, smarty pants."

"It's exactly the same as every other day of his little buggy life."

"Except that he's en route to London."

"Yes," Oliver says with a little frown. "Except for that."

One of the flight attendants appears in the dim aisle, a few dozen headsets strung from her arm like shoelaces.

She leans over the lady on the end with an exaggerated whisper. "Would either of you like one?" she asks, and they both shake their heads.

"I'm grand, thanks," Oliver says, and as she moves to the next row, he reaches into his pocket and emerges with his own earphones, unplugging them from his iPod. Hadley reaches below the seat for her backpack, rooting through it to find hers, too.

"Wouldn't want to miss the ducks," she jokes, but he's not listening. He's looking with interest at the pile of books and magazines she's set on her lap while digging through the bag.

"You obviously do read *some* good literature," he says, picking up the worn copy of *Our Mutual Friend*. He leafs through the pages carefully, almost reverently. "I love Dickens."

"Me, too," Hadley says. "But I haven't read this one."

"You should," Oliver tells her. "It's one of the best."

"So I've heard."

"*Some*body's certainly read it. Look at all these folded pages."

"It's my dad's," Hadley says with a little frown. "He gave it to me."

Oliver glances up at her, then closes the book on his lap. "And?"

"And I'm bringing it to London to give it back to him."

"Without having read it?"

"Without having read it."

"I'm guessing this is more complicated than it sounds."

Hadley nods. "You guessed right."

He'd given Hadley the book on their ski trip, the last time she'd seen him. On the way home, they'd been standing just outside the line for airport security when he'd reached into his bag and produced the thick black volume, the pages worn and yellowing, the dog-eared corners like missing jigsaw pieces.

"I thought you might like this one," he said, his smile tinged with desperation. Ever since Hadley had overheard his phone call to Charlotte, ever since she'd finally managed to put the pieces together, she'd barely spoken to him. All she could think about was getting home again, where she could curl up on the couch and put her head in her mother's lap and let loose all the tears she'd been holding back; all she wanted to do was cry and cry and cry until there was nothing left to cry about.

But there was Dad, with his unfamiliar beard and his new tweed jacket and his heart rooted somewhere across the ocean, his hand drooping beneath the weight of the book as he held it out to her. "Don't worry," he said with a feeble grin, "it's not poetry."

Hadley finally reached for it, looking down at the cover. There was no jacket, just the words etched across the black background: *Our Mutual Friend*.

"It's hard now," he said, his voice breaking just slightly. "I don't get to recommend books to you all that often. But certain ones are too important to get lost in all this." He waved a hand vaguely between them, as if to define just exactly what *this* was.

"Thanks," Hadley said, folding the book into her arms, hugging it to keep from hugging him. That they were left with only this—this awkward, prearranged meet-up, this terrible silence—seemed almost more than she could bear, and the unfairness of it all welled up inside of her. It was his fault, all of it, and yet her hatred for him was the worst kind of love, a tortured longing, a misguided wish that made her heart hammer in her chest. She couldn't ignore the disjointed sensation that they were now two different pieces of two different puzzles, and nothing in the world could make them fit together again.

"Come visit soon, okay?" he said, darting forward to give her a hug, and she nodded into his chest before pulling away. But she knew it would never happen. She had no intention of visiting him there. Even if she were open to the idea, as Mom and Dad both hoped she would be, the mathematics of it seemed utterly impossible to her. What was she supposed to do, spend Christmas there and Easter here? See her dad every other holiday and one week during the summer, just enough to glimpse his new life in fragments, tiny slivers of a world she had no part in? And all the while missing out on those moments of her mom's life—her mom, who'd done nothing to deserve to spend Christmas alone?

That, it seemed to Hadley, was no way to live. Perhaps if there were more time, or if time were more malleable; if she could be both places at once, live parallel lives; or, simpler yet, if Dad would just come home. Because as far as she was concerned, there was no in-between: She wanted all or nothing, illogically, irrationally, even though something inside of her knew that nothing would be too hard, and all was impossible.

After returning home from the ski trip she'd tucked the book away on a shelf in her room. But it wasn't long before she moved it again, stacking it beneath some others on the corner of her desk, and then again near the windowsill, the heavy volume skipping around her room like a stone until it eventually settled on the floor of her closet, where it had remained until this morning. And now here's Oliver shuffling through it, his fingers tripping across pages that haven't been opened in months.

"It's his wedding," Hadley says quietly. "My dad's."

Oliver nods. "Ah."

"Yeah."

"I'm guessing it's not a wedding gift, then."

"No," she says. "I'd say it's more of a gesture. Or maybe a protest."

"A Dickensian protest," he says. "Interesting."

"Something like that."

He's still idly thumbing through the pages, pausing every so often to scan a few lines. "Maybe you should reconsider."

"I can always get another at the library."

"I didn't just mean because of that."

"I know," she says, glancing down at the book again. She catches a flash of something as he leafs through, and she grabs his wrist without thinking. "Wait, stop."

He lifts his hands, and Hadley takes the book from his lap.

"I thought I saw something," she says, flipping back a few pages, her eyes narrowed. Her breath catches in her throat when she spots an underlined sentence, the line uneven, the ink faded. It's the simplest of markings: nothing written in the margin, no dog-eared page to flag it. Only a single line, hidden deep within the book, underscored by a wavery stroke of ink.

Even after all this time, even with all she's said to him and all she still hasn't, even in spite of her intention to return the book (because *that's* how you send a message, not with some unmarked, underlined quote in an old novel), Hadley's heart still flutters at the idea that perhaps she's been missing something important all this time. And now here it is on the page, staring up at her in plain black and white.

Oliver is looking at her, the question written all over his face, and so she murmurs the words out loud, running her finger along the line her father must have made.

"Is it better to have had a good thing and lost it, or never to have had it?"

When she glances up, their eyes meet for the briefest moment before they both look away again. Above them, the ducks are dancing on the screen, splashing along the edges of the pond, their happy little home, and Hadley lowers her chin to read the sentence again, this time to herself, then snaps the book shut and shoves it back into her bag.

Hadley in sleep: drifting, dreaming. In the small, faraway corners of her mind—humming, even as the rest of her has gone limp with exhaustion—she's on another flight, the one she missed, three hours farther along and seated beside a middle-aged man with a twitching mustache who sneezes and flinches his way across the Atlantic, never saying a word to her as she grows ever more anxious, her hand pressed against the window, where beyond the glass there is nothing but nothing but nothing.

She opens her eyes, awake all at once, to find Oliver's face just inches from her own, watchful and quiet, his expression unreadable. Hadley brings a hand to her heart, startled, before it registers that her head is on his shoulder.

"Sorry," she mumbles, pulling away. The plane is almost completely dark now, and it seems everyone on the flight is asleep. Even the television screens have gone black again, and Hadley pulls her tingling wrist from where it was wedged between them and squints at her watch, which is still, unhelpfully, on New York time. She runs a hand through her hair and then glances sideways at Oliver's shirt, relieved there's no sign of any drool, especially when he hands her a napkin.

"What's this for?"

He nods at it, and when she looks again, she sees that he's drawn one of the ducks from the movie.

"Is this your usual medium?" she asks. "Pen on napkin?"

He smiles. "I added the baseball cap and trainers so that he'd look more American."

"How thoughtful. Though we usually just call them sneakers," she says, the end of the sentence swallowed by a yawn. She tucks the napkin in the top of her bag. "You don't sleep on planes?"

He shrugs. "Normally I do."

"But not tonight?"

He shakes his head. "Apparently not."

"Sorry," she says again, but he waves it off.

"You looked peaceful."

"I don't *feel* peaceful," she says. "But it's probably good that I slept now, so I don't do it during the ceremony tomorrow."

Oliver looks at his own watch. "You mean today."

"Right," she says, then makes a face. "I'm a bridesmaid."

"That's nice."

"Not if I miss the ceremony."

"Well, there's always the reception."

"True," she says, yawning again. "I can't wait to sit all by myself and watch my dad dance with a woman I've never met before."

"You've never met her?" Oliver asks, his words tugged up at the end of the sentence by his accent.

"Nope."

"Wow," he says. "So I take it you aren't all that close?"

"Me and my dad? We used to be."

"And then?"

"And then your stupid country swallowed him whole."

Oliver laughs a small, uncertain laugh.

"He went over to teach for a semester at Oxford," Hadley explains. "And then he didn't come back."

"When?"

"Almost two years ago."

"And that's when he met this woman?"

"Bingo."

Oliver shakes his head. "That's awful."

"Yeah," Hadley says, a word far too insignificant to convey anything close to just how awful it was, just how awful it still *is*. But though she's told a longer version of the story a thousand times before to a thousand different people, she gets the feeling that Oliver might understand better than anyone else. It's something about the way he's looking at her, his eyes punching a neat little hole in her heart.

She's knows it's not real: It's the illusion of closeness, the false confidence of a hushed and darkened plane, but she doesn't mind. For the moment, at least, it feels real.

"You must've been shattered," he says. "And your mum, too."

"At first, yeah. She hardly got out of bed. But I think she bounced back quicker than I did."

"How?" he asks. "How do you bounce back from *that*?"

"I don't know," Hadley says truthfully. "She really believes that they're better off this way. That it was meant to work out like this. She has someone new and he has someone new and they're both happier now. It's just me who's not thrilled. Especially about meeting *his* someone new."

"Even though she's not so new anymore."

"*Especially* because she's not so new anymore. It makes it ten times more intense and awkward, and that's the last thing I want. I keep picturing walking into the reception all by myself and everyone staring at me. The melodramatic American daughter who refused to meet the new stepmother." Hadley crinkles her nose. "Stepmother. God."

Oliver frowns. "I think it's brave."

"What?"

"That you're going. That you're facing up to it. That you're moving on. It's brave."

"It doesn't feel that way."

"That's because you're in the middle of it," he says. "But you'll see."

She studies him carefully. "And what about you?"

"What *about* me?"

"I suppose you're not dreading yours half as much as I'm dreading mine?"

"Don't be too sure," he says stiffly. He'd been sitting close, his body angled toward hers, but now he moves away again, just barely, but enough so that she notices.

Hadley leans forward as he leans back, as if the two of them are joined by some invisible force. It's not as if her father's wedding is a particularly cheery subject for her, and she told him about that, didn't she? "So will you get to see your parents while you're home?"

He nods.

"That'll be nice," she says. "Are you guys close?"

He opens his mouth, then closes it again when the beverage cart comes rolling down the aisle, the cans making bright noises as they clink against one another, the bottles rattling. The flight attendant steps on the brake once she's past their row, locking it into place, then turns her back to them to begin taking orders.

It happens quickly, so quickly that Hadley almost doesn't see it at all: Oliver reaches into the pocket of his jeans for a coin, which he thumbs into the aisle with a quick snap of his wrist. Then he reaches across the sleeping woman, grabbing the coin with his left hand and snaking his right one into the cart, emerging with two miniature bottles of Jack Daniel's wrapped in his fist. He tucks them into his pocket, along with the coin, just seconds before the flight attendant twists back in their direction.

"Can I get you anything?" she asks, her eyes sweeping across Hadley's stricken face, Oliver's flushed cheeks, and the old woman still snoring with vigor at the end of the row.

"I'm okay," Hadley manages.

"Me, too," Oliver says. "Cheers, though."

When the flight attendant is gone again, the cart moving safely away, Hadley stares at him openmouthed. He pulls the bottles out and hands one to her, then twists the cap off the other with a shrug.

"Sorry," he says. "I just thought if we were going to do the whole 'talking about our families' thing, a bit of whiskey might be in order."

Hadley blinks at the bottle in her hand. "You planning to work this off or something?"

Oliver cracks a smile. "Ten years' hard labor?"

"I was thinking something more along the lines of washing dishes," she jokes, passing the bottle back to him. "Or maybe carrying luggage."

"I'm assuming you'll make me do that anyway," he says. "Don't worry, I'll leave a tenner on the seat when I go. I didn't want a hassle, even though I'm eighteen and we must be closer to London than to New York at this point. You like whiskey?"

Hadley shakes her head.

"Have you ever tried it?"

"No."

"Give it a go," he says, offering it to her again. "Just a sip."

She unscrews the cap and brings the bottle to her

74

mouth, already grimacing as the smell reaches her nose, harsh and smoky and far too strong. The liquid burns her throat as it goes down, and she coughs hard, her eyes watering, then screws the cap on and hands the bottle back to him.

"It's like licking a campfire," she says, making a face. "That's awful."

Oliver laughs as he finishes off his bottle.

"Okay, so now you've got your whiskey," she says. "Does that mean we get to talk about your family?"

"Why do you care?"

"Why wouldn't I?"

He sighs, a sound that comes out almost like a groan. "Let's see," he says eventually. "I have three older brothers—"

"Do they all still live in England?"

"Right. Three older brothers who still live in England," he says, unscrewing the cap on the second bottle of whiskey. "What else? My dad wasn't happy when I chose Yale over Oxford, but my mum was really pleased because she went to uni in America, too."

"Is that why he didn't come over with you at the start of school?"

Oliver gives her a pained look, like he'd rather be anywhere but here, then finishes off the last of the whiskey. "You ask an awful lot of questions."

"I told you that my dad left us for another woman and that I haven't seen him in over a year," she says. "Come on. I'm pretty sure there's no family drama that could top that."

"You didn't tell me that," he says. "That you haven't seen him in so long. I thought you just hadn't met *her*."

Now it's Hadley's turn to fidget in her seat. "We talk on the phone," she says. "But I'm still too angry to see him."

"Does he know that?"

"That I'm angry?"

Oliver nods.

"Of course," she says, then tilts her head at him. "But we're not talking about me, remember?"

"I just find it interesting," he says, "that you're so open about it. Everyone's always wound up about something in my family, but nobody ever says anything."

"Maybe you'd be better off if you did."

"Maybe."

Hadley realizes they've been whispering, leaning close in the shadows cast by the yellow reading light of the man in front of them. It almost feels as if they're alone, as if they could be anywhere, on a park bench somewhere or in a restaurant, miles below, with their feet firmly on the ground. She's close enough to see a small scar above his eye, the ghost of a beard along his jawline, the astonishing length of his eyelashes. Without even really meaning to, she finds herself leaning away, and Oliver looks startled by her sudden movement.

"Sorry," he says, sitting up and pulling his hand back from the armrest. "I forgot you get claustrophobic. You must be dying."

"No," she says, shaking her head. "Actually, it hasn't been so bad."

He juts his chin at the window, where the shade's still pulled down. "I still think it would help if you could see outside. It feels small in here even to me with no windows."

"That's my dad's trick," Hadley tells him. "The first time it happened, he told me to imagine the sky. But that only helps when the sky's *above* you."

"Right," Oliver says. "Makes sense."

They both fall silent, studying their hands as the quiet stretches between them.

"I used to be afraid of the dark," Oliver says after a moment. "And not just when I was little. It lasted till I was nearly eleven."

Hadley glances over, not sure what to say. His face looks more boyish now, less angular, his eyes rounder. She has a sudden urge to put her hand over his, but she stops herself.

"My brothers teased me like mad, switching off the lights whenever I walked into a room and then howling about it. And my dad just *hated* it. He had absolutely no sympathy. I remember I'd go into my parents' bedroom in the middle of the night and he'd tell me to stop being such a little girl. Or he'd tell me stories about monsters in the wardrobe, just to wind me up. His only advice was always just 'Grow up.' A real gem, right?"

"Parents aren't always right about everything," Hadley says. "Sometimes it just takes a while to figure that out."

"But then there was this one night," he continues, "when I

woke up and he was plugging in a night-light next to my bed. I'm sure he thought I was asleep, or else he'd never be caught dead, but I didn't say anything, just watched him plug it in and switch it on so there was this little circle of blue light."

Hadley smiles. "So he came around."

"In his own way, I guess," Oliver says. "But I mean, he must've bought it earlier in the day, right? He could've given it to me when he got back from the shop, or plugged it in before I went to bed. But he had to do it when nobody was watching." He turns to her, and she's struck by how sad he looks. "I'm not sure why I told you that."

"Because I asked," she says simply.

He draws in a jagged breath, and Hadley can see that his cheeks are flushed. The seat in front of her bobbles as the man readjusts the doughnut-shaped pillow around his neck. The cabin is quiet but for the hum of the air-conditioning, the soft flap of pages being turned, the occasional snuffling and shuffling of passengers trying their best to endure these last hours before landing. Every now and then a patch of turbulence sets the plane rocking gently, like a boat in a storm, and Hadley thinks again of her mother, of the awful things she said to her back in New York. Her eyes fall to the backpack at her feet, and not for the first time, she wishes they weren't somewhere over the Atlantic right now, so that she might try calling again.

Beside her, Oliver rubs his eyes. "I have a brilliant idea," he says. "How about we talk about something *other* than our parents?"

78

Hadley bobs her head. "Definitely."

But neither of them speaks. A minute ticks by, then another, and as the silence between them swells, they both begin to laugh.

"I'm afraid we might have to discuss the weather if you don't come up with something more interesting," he says, and Hadley raises her eyebrows.

"Me?"

He nods. "You."

"Okay," she says, cringing even before she's formed the words, but the question has been blooming inside of her for hours now, and the only thing to do, finally, is to ask it: "Do you have a girlfriend?"

Oliver's cheeks redden, and the smile she catches as he ducks his head is maddeningly cryptic; it is, Hadley decides, a smile with one of two meanings. The bigger part of her worries that it must be charitable, designed to make her feel less awkward about both the question and the coming answer, but something else keeps her wondering all the same: Maybe—just maybe—it's something even kinder than that, something full of understanding, a seal on the unspoken agreement between them that something is happening here, that this just might be a kind of beginning.

After a long moment, he shakes his head. "No girlfriend."

With this, it seems to Hadley that some sort of door has opened, but now that it finally has, she isn't quite sure how to proceed. "How come?"

He shrugs. "Haven't met anyone I want to spend fifty-two years with, I guess."

"There must be a million girls at Yale."

"Probably more like five or six thousand, actually."

"Mostly Americans, though, huh?"

Oliver smiles, then leans sideways, bumping her gently with his shoulder. "I like American girls," he says. "I've never dated one, though."

"That's not part of your summer research?"

He shakes his head. "Not unless the girl happens to be afraid of mayo, which, as you know, dovetails nicely with my study."

"Right," Hadley says, grinning. "So did you have a girlfriend in high school?"

"In secondary school, yes. She was nice. Quite fond of video games and pizza deliveries."

"Very funny," Hadley says.

"Well, I guess we can't all have epic loves at such a young age."

"So what happened to her?"

He tilts his head back against the seat. "What happened? I guess what always happens. We graduated. I left. We moved on. What happened to Mr. Pizza?"

"He did more than deliver pizzas, you know."

"Breadsticks, too?"

Hadley makes a face at him. "He broke up with me, actually."

"What happened?"

She sighs, adopting a philosophical tone. "What always happens, I guess. He saw me talking to another guy at a basketball game and got jealous, so he broke up with me over e-mail."

"Ah," Oliver says. "Epic love at its most tragic."

"Something like that," she agrees, looking over to find him watching her closely.

"He's an idiot."

"That's true," she says. "He was always sort of an idiot, in hindsight."

"Still," Oliver says, and Hadley smiles at him gratefully.

It was just after they'd broken up that Charlotte had called—in a display of phenomenal timing—to insist that Hadley bring a date to the wedding.

"Not everyone's getting a plus one," she'd explained, "but we thought it might be fun for you to have someone there with you."

"That's okay," Hadley said. "I'll be fine on my own."

"No, really," Charlotte insisted, completely oblivious to Hadley's tone. "It's no trouble at all. Besides," she said, her voice dropping to a conspiratorial whisper, "I heard you have a boyfriend."

In fact, Mitchell had broken up with her just three days earlier, and the drama of it was still tailing her through the halls at school with the persistence of some kind of invincible monster. It was something she didn't particularly want to discuss at all, much less with a future stepmother she'd never even met.

"You heard wrong," Hadley had said shortly. "I'll be okay flying solo."

The truth was, even if they *were* still dating, her father's wedding was pretty much the last place she'd ever be inclined to take somebody. Having to endure the night in a disaster of a bridesmaid dress while watching a bunch of adults do the "Y.M.C.A." would be hard enough to bear on her own; having company would only make it worse. The potential for secondhand embarrassment was sky-high: Dad and Charlotte kissing amid clinking glasses, stuffing cake into each other's faces, making overly cutesy speeches.

Hadley remembers thinking, when Charlotte extended the invitation all those months ago, that there was nobody in the world she hated enough to subject them to that. But now, looking at Oliver, she wonders if she got it wrong. She wonders if it was really that there had been nobody in the world she *liked* enough, nobody she felt so comfortable with that she'd allow them to witness this uneven milestone, this dreaded event. To her surprise, she has a fleeting image of Oliver in a tuxedo, standing at the door of a banquet hall, and as ridiculous as that is—the wedding isn't even black-tie—the idea of it makes her stomach flutter. She swallows hard, blinking away the thought.

Beside her, Oliver glances over at the old woman, still snoring in uneven rasps, her mouth twitching every now and then.

"I've actually got to use the loo," he admits, and Hadley nods.

"Me, too. I bet we can squeeze past her."

He unbuckles his seat belt and half stands in a jerky motion, bumping into the seat in front of him and eliciting a dirty look from the woman seated there. Hadley watches as he tries to maneuver past the old lady without waking her, and when they've both managed to make it out of their row, she follows him down the aisle and toward the back of the plane. A bored-looking flight attendant in a folded-down jump seat looks up from her magazine as they pass.

The OCCUPIED lights are on above both bathroom doors, so Hadley and Oliver stand in the small square of space just outside. They're close enough that she can smell the fabric of his shirt, the whiskey still on his breath; not so close that they're touching, exactly, but she can feel the hair on his arm tickle hers, and she's again seized by a sudden longing to reach for his hand.

She lifts her chin to find that he's looking down at her with the same expression she saw on his face earlier, when she woke up with her head on his shoulder. Neither of them moves and neither speaks; they just stand there watching each other in the darkness, the engines whirring beneath their feet. It occurs to her that—impossibly, improbably—he might be about to kiss her, and she inches just the tiniest bit closer, her heart skidding around in her chest. His hand brushes against hers, and Hadley feels it like a bolt of electricity, the shock of it moving straight up her spine. To her surprise, Oliver doesn't pull away;

instead, he fits his hand into hers as if anchoring her there, then tugs gently, moving her closer.

It almost feels as if they're completely alone—no captain or crew, no rows of dozing passengers stretching the length of the plane—and Hadley takes a deep breath and tips her head to look up at him. But then the door to one of the bathrooms is suddenly thrown open, bathing them in a too-bright wedge of light, and a little boy walks out trailing a long ribbon of toilet paper from one of his red shoes. And just like that, the moment is over.

7

Hadley wakes suddenly, without even realizing she'd been sleeping again. The cabin is still mostly dark, but the edges of the windows are now laced with daylight, and all around them people are beginning to stir, yawning and stretching and passing trays of rubbery bacon and eggs back across to the flight attendants, who look impossibly fresh and remarkably unwrinkled after such a long trip.

Oliver's head is resting on *her* shoulder this time, pinning Hadley into place, and when her attempt to stay perfectly still instead results in a kind of twitchy tremor that sets her arm in motion, he lurches up as if he's been shocked.

"Sorry," they say at the exact same time, then Hadley says it again: "Sorry."

Oliver rubs his eyes like a child awakening from a bad dream, then blinks at her, staring for just a beat too long. Hadley tries not to take it personally, but she knows she must look awful this morning. Earlier, when she stood in the tiny bathroom and regarded herself in the even tinier mirror, she'd been surprised to see how pale she looked, her eyes puffy from the stale air and high altitude.

She'd squinted at her reflection, marveling at the fact that Oliver was bothering with her at all. She wasn't normally the kind of girl to worry too much about hair and makeup, and she didn't tend to spend a lot of time in front of the mirror, but she was small and blond and pretty enough in the ways that seemed to count for the boys at her school. Still, the image in the mirror had been somewhat alarming, and that was before she'd nodded off for the second time. She can't imagine what she must look like now. Every inch of her feels achy with exhaustion, and her eyes sting; there's a soda stain near the collar of her shirt, and she's almost afraid to discover what might be going on with her hair at the moment.

But Oliver looks different, too; it's odd, seeing him in daylight, like switching the channel to high-definition. His eyes are still caked with sleep and there's a line running from his cheek to his temple where it was pressed against her shirt. But it's more than that; he looks pale and tired and drained, his eyes red-rimmed and somehow very faraway.

He arches his back in a stretch, then squints blearily at his watch. "Almost there."

Hadley nods, relieved that they're right on schedule, though a part of her also can't help wishing for more time. In spite of everything—the crowded quarters and the cramped seats, the smells that have been drifting up and down the length of the cabin for hours now—she doesn't feel quite ready to step off this plane, where it's been so easy to lose herself in conversation, to forget all that she left behind and all that's still ahead.

The man in front of them pushes open his window shade and a column of whiteness—so startlingly bright that Hadley brings a hand to her eyes—streams in all around them, snuffing out the darkness, stripping away whatever was left of last night's magic. Hadley reaches over to nudge open her own window shade, the spell now officially broken. Outside, the sky is a blinding blue, striped with clouds like layers on a cake. After so many hours in the dark, it almost hurts to look for too long.

It's only four AM in New York, and when the pilot's voice comes over the PA it sounds far too cheerful for the early hour. "Well, folks," he says, "we're making our final descent into Heathrow. The weather looks good down in London; twenty-two degrees and partly sunny with a chance of showers later. We'll be on the ground in just under twenty minutes, so please fasten your seat belts. It's been a pleasure flying with you, and I hope you enjoy your stay."

Hadley turns to Oliver. "What's that in Fahrenheit?"

"Warm," he says, and in that moment she feels too warm herself; perhaps it's the forecast, or the sun beating at the

87

window, or maybe just the proximity of the boy at her side, his shirt wrinkled and his cheeks a ruddy pink. She stretches to reach the nozzle on the panel above her, twisting it all the way to the left and then closing her eyes against the thin jet of cool air.

"So," he says, cracking his knuckles one at a time.

"So."

They look at each other sideways, and something about the expression on his face—an uncertainty that mirrors her own—makes Hadley want to cry. There's no real distinction between last night and this morning, of course—just dark bleeding into light—but even so, everything feels horribly different. She thinks of the way they stood together near the bathroom, how it seemed like they'd been on the brink of something, of *everything,* like the whole world was changing as they huddled together in the dark. And now here they are, like two polite strangers, like she'd only ever imagined the rest of it. She wishes they could turn around again and fly back in the other direction, circling the globe backward, chasing the night they left behind.

"Do you think," she says, the words emerging thickly, "we might have used up all our conversation last night?"

"Not possible," says Oliver, and the way he says it, his mouth turned up in a smile, his voice full of warmth, unwinds the knot in Hadley's stomach. "We haven't even gotten to the really important stuff yet."

"Like what?" she asks, trying to arrange her face in a

way that disguises the relief she feels. "Like what's so great about Dickens?"

"Not at all," he says. "More like the plight of koalas. Or the fact that Venice is sinking." He pauses, waiting for this to register, and when Hadley says nothing, he slaps his knee for emphasis. "Sinking! The whole city! Can you believe it?"

She frowns in mock seriousness. "That does sound pretty important."

"It *is*," Oliver insists. "And don't even get me started on the size of our carbon footprint after this trip. Or the difference between crocodiles and alligators. Or the longest recorded flight of a chicken."

"Please tell me you don't actually know that."

"Thirteen seconds," he says, leaning forward to look past her and out the window. "This is a total disaster. We're nearly to Heathrow and we haven't even properly discussed flying chickens." He jabs a finger at the window. "And see those clouds?"

"Hard to miss," Hadley says; the plane is now almost fully enveloped in fog, the grayness pressing up against the windows as the plane dips lower and lower.

"Those are cumulus clouds. Did you know that?"

"I'm sure I should."

"They're the best ones."

"How come?"

"Because they look the way clouds are supposed to look, the way you draw them when you're a kid. Which is nice, you know? I mean, the sun never looks the way you drew it."

"Like a wheel with spokes?"

"Exactly. And my family certainly never looked the way I drew them."

"Stick figures?"

"Come on now," he says. "Give me a little credit. They had hands and feet, too."

"That looked like mittens?"

"But it's nice, isn't it? When something matches up like that?" He bobs his head with a satisfied smile. "Cumulus clouds. Best clouds ever."

Hadley shrugs. "I guess I never really thought about it."

"Well, then, see?" Oliver says. "There's loads more to talk about. We've only just gotten started."

Beyond the window the clouds are bottoming out, and the plane lowers itself gently into the silvery sky below. Hadley feels a rush of illogical relief at the sight of the ground, though it's still too far away to make any sense, just a collection of quilted fields and shapeless buildings, the faint tracings of roads running through them like gray threads.

Oliver yawns and leans his head back against the seat. "I guess we probably should have slept more," he says. "I'm pretty knackered."

Hadley gives him a blank look.

"Tired," he says, flattening the vowels and notching his voice up an octave so that he sounds American, though his accent has a vaguely Southern twang to it.

"I feel like I've embarked on some kind of foreign-language course."

"Learn to speak British in just seven short hours!" Oliver says in his best announcer's voice. "How could you pass up an advert like that?"

"Commercial," she says, rolling her eyes. "How could you pass up a *commercial* like that?"

But Oliver only grins. "See how much you've learned already?"

They've nearly forgotten the old woman beside them, who's been sleeping for so long that it's the absence of her muffled snoring that finally startles them into looking over.

"What did I miss?" she asks, reaching for her purse, from which she carefully removes her glasses, a bottle of eye drops, and the small tin of mints.

"We're almost there," Hadley tells her. "But you're lucky you slept. It was a *long* flight."

"It was," Oliver says, and though he's facing away from her, Hadley can hear the smile in his voice. "It felt like forever."

The woman stops what she's doing, the eyeglasses dangling between her thumb and forefinger, and beams at them. "I told you," she says simply, then returns to the contents of her purse. Hadley, feeling the full meaning of her statement, avoids Oliver's searching look as the flight attendants do one last sweep of the aisle, reminding people to put their seat backs up, fasten their safety belts, and tuck away their bags.

"Looks like we could even be a few minutes early," Oliver says. "So unless customs is a complete nightmare, you might actually have a shot at making this thing. Where's the wedding?"

Hadley leans forward and pulls the Dickens book from her bag again, slipping the invitation out from near the back, where she has pressed it for safekeeping. "The Kensington Arms Hotel," she says. "Sounds swanky."

Oliver leans over to look at the elegant calligraphy scrawled across the cream-colored invitation. "That's the reception," he says, pointing just above it. "The ceremony's at St Barnabas Church."

"Is that close?"

"To Heathrow?" He shakes his head. "Not exactly. But nothing really is. You should be okay if you hurry."

"Where's yours?"

His jaw tightens. "Paddington."

"Where's that?"

"Near where I grew up," he says. "West London."

"Sounds nice," she offers, but he doesn't smile.

"It's the church we used to go to as kids," he says. "I haven't been there in ages. I used to always get in trouble for climbing the statue of Mary out front."

"Nice," Hadley says, tucking the wedding invitation back inside the book and then shutting it a bit too hard, causing Oliver to flinch. He watches her shove it back into her bag.

"So will you still give it back to him?"

"I don't know," she says truthfully. "Probably."

He considers this for a moment. "Will you at least wait till after the wedding?"

92

Hadley hadn't planned on it. In fact, she'd envisioned herself marching right up to him before the ceremony and handing it over, mutinously, triumphantly. It was the only thing he'd given her since he left—really *given* her; not a gift mailed out for her birthday or Christmas, but something he'd handed to her himself—and there was something satisfying in the idea of giving it right back. If she was going to be made to attend his stupid wedding, then she was going to do it her way.

But Oliver is watching her with a look of great earnestness, and she can't help feeling a bit uncomfortable beneath his hopeful gaze. Her voice wavers when she answers. "I'll think about it," she says, then adds, "I might not get there in time anyway."

Their eyes drift to the window to chart their progress, and Hadley pushes down a wave of panic; not so much for the landing itself, but for all that begins and ends with it. Out the window, the ground is rushing up to meet them, making everything—all the blurry shapes below— suddenly clear, the churches and the fences and the fast-food restaurants, even the scattered sheep in an isolated field, and she watches it all draw closer, wrapping a hand tightly around her seat belt, bracing herself as if arriving were no better than crashing.

The wheels hit the ground with one bounce, then two, before the velocity of the landing pins them firmly to the runway and they're shot forward like a blown cork, all wind and engines and rushing noise, and a sense of momentum so strong that Hadley wonders if they'll be able to stop at all. But they do, of course they do, and everything goes quiet again; after traveling nearly five hundred miles per hour for almost seven hours, they now commence crawling to the gate with all the unhurried speed of an apple cart.

Their runway fans out to join others like a giant maze, until they're all swallowed by an apron of asphalt stretching as far as Hadley can see, interrupted only by radio towers and rows of planes and the great hulking terminal, which sits bleakly beneath the low gray sky. *So this is London,* she thinks. Her back is still to Oliver, but she finds herself glued to the window by some invisible force, unable to turn and face him without quite knowing why.

As they pull up to the gate, she can see the ramp stretched out to meet them, and the plane slips into position gracefully, locking on with a small shudder. But even once they're firmly anchored in place, once the engines are cut and the seat-belt lights go off with a *ping,* Hadley remains still. There's a collective hum of noise at her back as the rest of the passengers stand to collect their baggage, and Oliver waits a moment before lightly touching her arm. She whirls around.

"Ready?" he asks, and she shakes her head, just barely, but enough to make him smile. "Me, neither," he admits, standing up anyway.

Just before it's their turn to file out of the row, Oliver reaches into his pocket and pulls out a purplish bill. He sets it on the seat he's been occupying for the past seven hours, where it sits limply, looking a bit lost against the busy pattern of the cloth.

"What's that for?" Hadley asks.

"The whiskey, remember?"

"Right," she says, peering closer. "There's no way it was worth twenty pounds, though."

He shrugs. "Thievery surcharge."

"What if someone takes it?"

Oliver bends down and grabs both ends of the seat belt, which he fastens over the bill so that it looks as if it's tucked in. "There," he says, standing back to admire his work. "Safety first."

Ahead of them, the old woman takes a few small, bird-like steps out into the aisle before pausing to peer up at the overhead bins. Oliver moves quickly to help, ignoring the crowd of people behind them as he pulls down her battered suitcase and then waits patiently while she gets herself situated.

"Thank you," she says, beaming at him. "You're such a nice boy." She moves to begin walking, then hesitates, as if she's forgotten something, and looks back again. "You remind me of my husband," she says to Oliver, who shakes his head in protest. But the woman has already begun to pivot around again, in a series of tiny, incremental steps, like the minute hand on a clock, and when she's finally pointed in the right direction she begins her slow shuffle up the aisle, leaving the two of them to watch her go.

"Hope that was a compliment," Oliver says, looking a bit sheepish.

"They've been married fifty-two years," Hadley reminds him.

He gives her a sideways glance as she reaches for her suitcase. "Thought you didn't think much of marriage."

"I don't," she says, heading toward the exit.

When he catches up to her on the walkway, neither of them says a word, but Hadley feels it anyway, bearing down on them like a freight train: the moment when they'll have to say good-bye. And for the first time in hours, she feels suddenly shy. Beside her, Oliver is craning his neck to read the signs for customs, already thinking about the next thing, already moving on. Because that's what you do on planes. You share an armrest with someone for a few hours. You exchange stories about your life, an amusing anecdote or two, maybe even a joke. You comment on the weather and remark about the terrible food. You listen to him snore. And then you say good-bye.

So why does she feel so completely unprepared for this next part?

She should be worrying about finding a taxi and making it to the church on time, seeing her dad again and meeting Charlotte. But what she's thinking about instead is Oliver, and this realization—this reluctance to let go—throws everything into sudden doubt. What if she's gotten it all wrong, these last hours? What if it isn't as she thought?

Already, everything is different. Already, Oliver feels a million miles away.

When they reach the end of the corridor they're greeted by the tail end of a long queue, where their fellow passengers stand with bags strewn at their feet, restless and grumbling. As she drops her backpack, Hadley does a mental tally of all that she packed inside, trying to remember whether she threw in a pen that could be used to capture a phone number or an e-mail address, some scrap of information about him, an insurance policy against forgetting. But she feels frozen inside of herself, trapped by her inability to say anything that won't come out sounding vaguely desperate.

Oliver yawns and stretches, his hands high and his back arched, then drops his elbow casually onto her shoulder, pretending to use her for support. But the weight of his arm feels like it just might be the thing to unbalance her, and she swallows hard before looking up at him, uncharacteristically flustered.

"Are you taking a cab?" she asks, and he shakes his head and reclaims his arm.

"Tube," he says. "It's not far from the station."

Hadley wonders whether he's talking about the church or his house, whether he's heading home to shower and change or going straight to the wedding. She hates the fact that she won't know. It feels like the last day of school, the final night at summer camp, like everything is coming to an abrupt and dizzying end.

To her surprise, he lowers his face so it's level with hers, then narrows his eyes and touches a finger lightly to her cheek.

"Eyelash," he says, rubbing his thumb to get rid of it.

"What about my wish?"

"I made it for you," he says with a smile so crooked it makes her heart dip.

Is it possible she's only known him for ten hours?

"I wished for a speedy trip through customs," he tells her. "Otherwise, you don't have a shot in hell at making this thing."

Hadley glances at the clock on the concrete wall above them and realizes he's right; it's already 10:08, less than two hours before the wedding is scheduled to begin. And here she is, stuck in customs, her hair tangled and her dress wadded up in her bag. She tries to picture herself walking down the aisle, but something about the image refuses to match up with her current state.

She sighs. "Does this usually take long?"

"Not now that I've made my wish," Oliver says, and then, as if it were just that simple, the line begins to move. He gives her a triumphant look as he steps forward, and Hadley trails after him, shaking her head.

"If that's all it takes, you couldn't have wished for a million dollars?"

"A million pounds," he says. "You're in London now. And no. Who'd want to deal with the taxes?"

"What taxes?"

"On your million pounds. At least eighty-eight percent of that would probably go straight to the Queen."

Hadley gives him a long look. "Eighty-eight percent, huh?"

"The numbers never lie," he says with a grin.

When they reach the point where the line forks, they're greeted by a joyless customs official in a blue suit who's leaning against the metal railing and pointing to a sign that indicates which direction they're meant to go.

"EU citizens to the right, all others to the left," he repeats over and over again, his voice thin and reedy and mostly lost to the thrum of the crowd. "EU citizens to the right…"

Hadley and Oliver exchange a look, and all her uncertainty disappears. Because it's there in his face, a fleeting reluctance that matches her own. They stand there together for a long time, for too long, for what seems like forever, each unwilling to part ways, letting the people behind them stream past like a river around rocks.

"Sir," says the customs official, breaking off mid-mantra to put a hand on Oliver's back, shepherding him forward, urging him away. "I'm going to have to ask you to keep moving so you don't hold up the line."

"Just one minute—" Oliver begins, but he's cut off.

"Sir, *now*," the man says, directing him a little bit more insistently.

A woman with a hiccupping baby is trying to push past Hadley, shoving her forward in the process, and there seems to be nothing to do but let herself be borne along by the current. But before she can move any farther she feels a hand on her elbow, and just like that Oliver is beside her again. He looks down at her with his head tilted, his hand still firmly on her arm, and before she has a chance to be nervous, before she even fully realizes what's happening, she hears him mutter "What the hell," and then, to her surprise, he bends to kiss her.

The line continues to move around them and the customs official gives up for the moment with a frustrated sigh, but Hadley doesn't notice any of it; she grabs Oliver's shirt tightly, afraid of being swept away from him, but his hand is pressing on her back as he kisses her, and the truth is, she's never felt so safe in her life. His lips are soft and taste salty from the pretzels they shared earlier, and she closes her eyes—just for a moment—and the rest of the world disappears. By the time he pulls away with a grin, she's too stunned to say anything. She stumbles backward a step as the customs guy hurries Oliver along in the other direction, rolling his eyes.

"It's not like the lines lead to separate countries," he mutters.

The concrete partition between the two areas is coming up fast between them, and Oliver lifts a hand to wave, still beaming at her. In a moment, Hadley realizes, she won't be able to see him at all, but she catches his eye and waves back. He points a finger toward the front of his line and she nods, hoping it means she'll see him out there, and then he's gone, and there's nothing to do but keep moving, her passport in hand, the feel of the kiss still lingering like a stamp on her lips. She puts a hand to her heart to calm the thudding.

But it's not long before she realizes Oliver's wish has failed to come true; her line is practically at a standstill, and sandwiched between a crying baby and a huge man in a Texas shirt, Hadley's never felt so impatient in her life. Her eyes dart from her watch to the wall behind which Oliver disappeared, and she counts out the minutes with a feverish intensity, squirming and fidgeting, pacing and sighing as she waits.

When it's finally her turn, she practically runs up to the glass window and shoves her passport through the slot.

"Business or pleasure?" the woman asks as she studies the little booklet, and Hadley hesitates before answering, since neither answer seems quite accurate. She settles on pleasure—though watching her father get married again can hardly be categorized that way—then fires off answers to the rest of the questions with enough gusto to make the woman eye her suspiciously before stamping one of the many blank pages in Hadley's passport.

Her suitcase rocks back and forth unsteadily as she hurries past the checkpoint and toward the baggage claim, deciding that the apple she grabbed from the fridge at home doesn't really count as a farm product. It's now 10:42, and if she doesn't manage to get a cab in the next few minutes there's pretty much no chance she'll make the ceremony. But she's not thinking about that yet. She's thinking only of Oliver, and when she emerges into the baggage area—a sea of people, all crowded behind a black rope, holding signs and waiting for friends and family—her heart sinks.

The room is enormous, with dozens of carousels bearing brightly colored suitcases, and all around them, fanned out in every direction, hundreds upon hundreds of people, each of them searching for something: for people or rides or directions, for things lost and found. Hadley wheels in a circle, her bags feeling like they weigh a thousand pounds, her shirt sticking to her back, her hair falling across her eyes. There are children and grandparents, limo drivers and airport officials, a guy with a Starbucks apron and three monks in red robes. A million people, it seems, and none of them Oliver.

She backs up against a wall and sets down her things, forgetting even to worry about the crush of people. Her mind is too busy with the possibilities. It could have been anything, really. His line could have taken longer. He could have been held up at customs. He might have emerged earlier and assumed that *she'd* gone ahead. They could have crossed paths and not even noticed.

He might simply have left.

But still, she waits.

The giant clock above the flight board stares down at her accusingly, and Hadley tries to ignore the mounting sense of panic that's ballooning inside her. How could he not have said good-bye? Or was that what he'd meant by the kiss? Still, after all those hours, all those moments between them, how could that just be it?

She realizes she doesn't even know his last name.

The very last place she wants to go right now is to a wedding. She can almost feel the last of her energy receding, like water spiraling down a drain. But as the minutes tick by, it's becoming harder to ignore the fact that she's going to miss the ceremony. With some amount of effort, she peels herself away from the wall to make one last sweep of the place, her feet heavy as she paces the enormous terminal; but Oliver, with his blue shirt and untidy hair, is nowhere to be found.

And so, with nothing more to be done, Hadley finally makes her way out through the sliding doors and into the gray London haze, feeling satisfied at least that the sun didn't have the audacity to show up this morning.

5:48 AM Eastern Standard Time
10:48 AM Greenwich Mean Time

The line for taxis is almost comically long, and Hadley drags her suitcase to the end of it with a groan, falling in behind a family of Americans wearing matching red T-shirts and talking much too loud. Heathrow has turned out to be no less busy than JFK, though without the Fourth of July as an excuse, and she waits numbly as the line creeps forward, the lack of sleep finally beginning to catch up to her. Everything seems to blur as her gaze moves from the queue ahead of her to the departing buses to the line of black taxis waiting their turn, as solemn and silent as a funeral procession.

"It can't be worse than New York," she'd said earlier when Oliver had warned her about Heathrow, but he only shook his head

"A logistics nightmare of epic proportions," he'd called it, and of course he'd been right.

She gives her head a little shake, as if trying to rid her ear of water. *He's gone,* she tells herself again. *It's just as simple as that.* But even so, she keeps her back to the terminal, resisting the urge to turn around and look for him one more time.

Someone once told her there's a formula for how long it takes to get over someone, that it's half as long as the time you've been together. Hadley has her doubts about how accurate this could possibly be, a calculation so simple for something as complicated as heartbreak. After all, her parents had been married almost twenty years, and it took Dad only a few short months to fall for someone else. And when Mitchell had dumped Hadley after a whole semester, it took her only about ten days to feel done with him entirely. Still, she takes comfort in the knowledge that she's known Oliver for only a matter of hours, meaning this knot in her chest should be gone by the end of the day, at the very latest.

When it's finally her turn at the front of the line, she digs through her bag for the address of the church while the cabbie—a tiny man with a beard so long and white that he looks a bit like a garden gnome—tosses her suitcase roughly into the trunk without so much as a pause in conversation as he jabbers away into his hands-free phone. Once again, Hadley tries not to think about the condition of the dress she'll soon be forced to put on. She hands over

106

the address and the cabbie climbs back into the car without any sort of acknowledgment of his new passenger.

"How long will it take?" she asks as she slips into the backseat, and he halts his steady chatter just long enough to let out a sharp bark of a laugh.

"Long time," he says, then pulls out into the slow crawl of traffic.

"Super," Hadley says under her breath.

Out the window, the landscape scrolls by from behind a gauzy layer of mist and rain. There's a grayness here that seems to hang over everything, and even though the wedding will be indoors, Hadley finds herself softening toward Charlotte for a moment; anybody would be disappointed with this sort of weather on her wedding day, even if she was British and had spent a lifetime learning not to expect anything else. There's always that tiny piece of hope that this day—*your* day—will be the one to turn out differently.

When the cab pulls onto the motorway, the low-slung buildings start to give way to narrow brick homes, which stand shoulder to shoulder amid spindly antennae and cluttered yards. Hadley wants to ask whether this is part of London proper, but she has a feeling her driver would be a less than enthusiastic tour guide. If Oliver were here, he'd undoubtedly be telling her stories about everything they passed, though there'd be enough outlandish tales and not-quite-truths sprinkled in there to keep her on her toes, too, to make her wonder whether any of it was really true at all.

On the plane he'd told her about trips to South Africa and Argentina and India with his family, and Hadley had folded her arms as she listened, wishing she were on her way to somewhere like that. It wasn't such a leap, from where she was sitting. There on the plane, it wasn't so very hard to imagine they could be headed somewhere together.

"Which was your favorite?" she'd asked. "Of all the places you've been?"

He seemed to consider this for a moment before that one telltale dimple appeared on his face. "Connecticut."

Hadley laughed. "I bet," she said. "Who'd want to go to Buenos Aires when you could see New Haven?"

"What about you?"

"Alaska, probably. Or Hawaii."

Oliver looked impressed. "Not bad. The two most far-flung states."

"I've been to all but one, actually."

"You're kidding."

Hadley shook her head. "Nope, we used to take a lot of family road trips when I was younger."

"So you drove to Hawaii? How was that?"

She grinned. "We thought it made more sense to fly to that one, actually."

"So which one have you missed?"

"North Dakota."

"How come?"

She shrugged. "Just haven't made it there yet, I guess."

"I wonder how long it would take to drive there from Connecticut."

Hadley laughed. "Can you even drive on the right side of the road?"

"Yes," Oliver said, flashing her a look of mock anger. "I know it's shocking to think that I might be able to operate a vehicle on the *wrong* side of the road, but I'm actually quite good. You'll see when we take our big road trip to North Dakota one day."

"I can't wait," Hadley said, reminding herself that it was only a joke. Still, the idea of the two of them crossing the country together, listening to music as the horizon rolled past, had been enough to make her smile.

"So what's your favorite place *outside* of the States?" he asked. "I know it's absurd to think there might be somewhere else in the world as wonderful as, say, New Jersey, but..."

"This is my first time overseas, actually."

"Really?"

She nodded.

"Lot of pressure, then."

"On what?"

"London."

"My expectations aren't particularly high."

"Fair enough," he said. "So if you could go anywhere else in the world, where would it be?"

Hadley thought about this for a moment. "Maybe Australia. Or Paris. How about you?"

Oliver had looked at her as if it were obvious, the faintest hint of a grin at the corners of his mouth.

"North Dakota," he'd said.

Now Hadley presses her forehead against the window of the taxi and once again finds herself smiling at the thought of him. He's like a song she can't get out of her head. Hard as she tries, the melody of their meeting runs through her mind on an endless loop, each time as surprisingly sweet as the last, like a lullaby, like a hymn, and she doesn't think she could ever get tired of hearing it.

She watches with bleary eyes as the world rushes past, and tries her best to stay awake. Her phone rings four times before she realizes it's not the cabbie's, and when she finally fishes it out of her bag and sees that it's her dad, she hesitates for a moment before answering.

"I'm in a taxi," she says by way of greeting, then cranes her neck to check the clock on the dashboard. Her stomach does a little somersault when she sees that it's already 11:24.

Dad sighs, and Hadley imagines him in his tux, pacing the halls of the church. She wonders if he wishes she hadn't come after all. There are so many more important things for him to be worrying about today—flowers and programs and seating arrangements—that Hadley's missed flight and the fact that she's running late must seem more of a headache than anything else.

"Do you know if you're close?" he asks, and she covers the mouthpiece and clears her throat loudly. The driver flinches, quite obviously annoyed at being interrupted.

"Excuse me, sir," she says. "Do you know how far now?"

He puffs out his cheeks, then heaves a sigh. "Twenty minutes," he says. "Thirty. Eh, twenty-five. Thirty, maybe. Thirty."

Hadley frowns and returns the phone to her ear. "I think maybe a half hour."

"Damn it," Dad says. "Charlotte's gonna have a stroke."

"You can start without me."

"It's a wedding, Hadley," he says. "It's not like skipping the previews at the cinema."

Hadley bites her lip to keep from saying "movie theater."

"Look," Dad says, "tell the driver you'll give him an extra twenty quid if he can get you here in twenty minutes. I'll talk to the minister and see if we can stall for a bit, okay?"

"Okay," she says, looking doubtfully at the driver.

"And don't worry—Charlotte's friends are on standby," Dad says, and Hadley can once again hear the humor in his voice, that trace of laughter behind his words that she remembers from when she was little.

"For what?"

"For you," he says cheerfully. "See you soon."

The driver seems to perk up quite a bit at the idea of a bonus, and after striking a bargain he turns off the motorway and onto a series of smaller roads lined with colorful buildings, an assortment of pubs and markets and little boutiques. Hadley wonders if she should try to start getting ready in the car, but this seems far too daunting an endeavor, and so instead she just looks out the window, biting her fingernails and trying not to think about anything at all. It seems almost easier to go into this blindfolded. Like a man about to be shot.

She glances down at the phone in her lap, then flips it open to try to call her mom. But it goes straight to voice mail, and she snaps it shut again with a heavy feeling. A quick calculation tells her it's still early in Connecticut, and Mom—being a bear of a sleeper, completely oblivious to the world until she's had a shower and a massive amount of coffee—is probably still in bed. Somehow, despite their uneven parting, Hadley suspects her mother's voice might be just the thing to make her feel better, and she wishes for nothing more than to hear it right now.

The cabbie is true to his word; at exactly 11:46, they pull up to an enormous church with a red roof and a steeple so high the very top of it is lost to the mist. The front doors are open, and two round-faced men in tuxes hover in the doorway.

Hadley sifts through the stack of brightly colored bills her mom exchanged for her, handing over what seems like an awful lot for a ride from the airport, plus the extra twenty she promised, which leaves her with only ten pounds. After stepping out into the rain to heave her suitcase from the trunk, the driver pulls away in the taxi, and Hadley simply stands there for a moment, peering up at the church.

From inside she can hear the deep peals of an organ,

and in the doorway the two ushers shuffle their stacks of programs and smile at her expectantly. But she spots another door along the brick wall out front and sets off in that direction instead. The only thing worse than walking down the aisle would be to accidentally do it too early, wearing a wrinkled jean skirt and toting a red suitcase.

The door leads to a small garden with a stone statue of a saint, currently occupied by three pigeons. Hadley wheels her suitcase along the side of the building until she comes across another door, and when she shoves it open with her shoulder the sound of the music fills the garden. She looks right and then left down the hallway before taking off toward the back of the church, where she runs into a small woman wearing a little hat with feathers.

"Sorry," Hadley says, half whispering. "I'm looking for...the groom?"

"Ah, you must be Hadley!" the woman says. "I'm so glad you made it. Don't worry, dear. The girls are waiting for you downstairs." She says *girls* as if it rhymes with *carols,* and Hadley realizes this must be the bride's mother, from Scotland. Now that Dad and Charlotte are getting married, Hadley wonders if she's supposed to consider this woman—this total stranger—a grandmother of sorts. She's struck a bit speechless by the idea of it, wondering what other new family members she might be acquiring once the day's events are set in motion. But before she has a chance to say anything, the woman makes a little flapping motion with her hands.

"Better hurry," she says, and Hadley finds her voice again, thanking her quickly before heading toward the stairwell.

As she bumps her suitcase down one step at a time, she can hear a flurry of voices, and by the time she hits the bottom, she's completely surrounded.

"*There* she is," one of the women says, putting an arm around her shoulders to shepherd her into a Sunday-school classroom that appears to be doubling as a dressing room. Another grabs her suitcase, and a third guides her into a folding chair, which is set up in front of the mirror that leans against the chalkboard. All four women are already wearing their lavender bridesmaid dresses, and their hair is sprayed, their eyebrows plucked, their makeup done. Hadley tries to keep them straight as they introduce themselves, but it's clear that there's very little time for pleasantries; these women are all business.

"We thought you might miss it," says Violet, the maid of honor, a childhood friend of Charlotte's. She flits around Hadley's head, taking a clip from her mouth. Another, Jocelyn, grabs a makeup brush and then squints for a moment before getting to work. In the mirror, Hadley can see that the other two have opened her suitcase and are attempting to smooth out the dress, which is as hopelessly wrinkled as she feared.

"Don't worry, don't worry," says Hillary, disappearing into the bathroom with it. "It's the kind of dress where the creases just give it a little life."

"How was your flight?" Violet asks as she jams a brush

through Hadley's hair, which is still tangled from the hours spent on the plane. Before Hadley has a chance to answer, Violet twists her hair into a knot, pulling so hard that Hadley's blue eyes nearly disappear.

"Too tight," she manages, feeling like Snow White, getting pecked to death by too many helpful forest creatures.

But by the time they're done with her a mere ten minutes later, Hadley has to admit they've pulled off some sort of miracle. The dress, while still a bit squashed, looks better than it ever did when she tried it on back home, thanks to Mom's last-minute triage yesterday morning and some creative pinning by her fellow bridesmaids. The spaghetti straps are the perfect length and the lavender silk hangs just right, ending at her knees. The shoes are Mom's, strappy sandals as shiny as two coins, and Hadley wiggles her painted toes as she studies them. Her hair is pulled back into an elegant bun, and between that and the makeup, she feels completely unlike herself.

"You look like a ballerina," Whitney says, clasping her hands together delightedly, and Hadley smiles, a bit shy amid so many fairy godmothers. But even she has to admit that it's true.

"We better go," Violet says, glancing up at the clock, which reads 12:08. "Don't want Charlotte to have a heart attack on her wedding day."

The others laugh as they take one last look in the mirror, then the whole group hurries out the door as one, their heels loud on the linoleum floor of the church basement.

But Hadley finds herself frozen in place. It's only just occurred to her that she won't have a chance to see her father before the ceremony, and something about this sets her completely off-balance. All of a sudden everything seems to be happening much too fast, and she smoothes her dress and bites her lip and tries unsuccessfully to slow her rushing mind.

He's getting married, she thinks, marveling at the very idea of it. *Married.*

All this she's known for months—that he's starting a new life today, a life with someone who's not Mom—but until now it was only ever just words, the vaguest of notions, the kind of future occasion that seems like it might not ever actually happen, that sneaks up on you like the monsters in childhood stories, all fur and teeth and claws, without any real substance.

But now, standing here in the basement of a church with shaking hands and a hammering heart, she's struck by what this day actually means, by all that she'll lose and gain with it, by how much has already changed. And something inside of her begins to hurt.

One of the bridesmaids calls from down the hall, where the echoing of footsteps is growing softer. Hadley takes a deep breath, trying to remember what Oliver said on the plane about her being brave. And though at this particular moment she feels quite the opposite, something in the memory makes her stand up a bit taller, and so she holds on to this as she sets off after the group, her eyes wide under her makeup.

Upstairs, she's led around to the lobby at the front of the church and introduced to Charlotte's brother, Monty, who will be the one walking her down the aisle. He's rail thin and ghostly pale, and Hadley guesses he's at least a few years older than Charlotte, putting him on the other side of forty. He offers her a hand, which is cold and papery, and then, once the introductions have been made, proffers his elbow. Someone hands her a pink and lavender bouquet as they're maneuvered into line behind the others, and before she can even really register what's happening the doors are thrown open and the eyes of the congregation are suddenly upon them.

When it's their turn Monty nudges her forward, and Hadley walks with small steps, a bit unsteady in her heels. The wedding is bigger than she'd imagined; for months she's been picturing a small country church filled with a few close friends. But this is nothing short of a gala event, and there are hundreds of unfamiliar faces, all turned in her direction.

She adjusts her grip on the stems of the bouquet and lifts her chin. On the groom's side, she spots a few people she vaguely knows: an old college friend of her father's; a second cousin who's been living in Australia; and an elderly uncle who for years sent her birthday gifts on the completely wrong day, and who—if she's being really honest—she sort of assumed was dead by now.

As they make their way up the aisle, Hadley has to remind herself to breathe. The music is loud in her ears and the dim lighting of the church makes her blink. It's hard to tell whether she's warm because there's no air-conditioning or because of the panicky feeling she's trying hard to push away, that familiar sensation that comes with too many people in too little space.

When they're finally near the front of the church, she's startled to see her dad standing at the altar. It seems faintly ridiculous that he should be up there at all, in this church in London that smells of rain and perfume, a line of women in purple dresses making their way toward him with halting steps. It doesn't fit somehow, this image of him before her, clean-shaven and bright-eyed, a small purple flower pinned to his lapel. It seems to Hadley that there are a thousand more likely places for him to be at the moment, on this summer afternoon. He should be in their kitchen back home, wearing those ratty pajamas of his, the ones with the holes in the heels where the legs are too long. Or flipping through a stack of bills in his old office, sipping tea from his GOT POETRY? mug, thinking about heading outside to mow the lawn. There are, in fact, any number of things he should be doing right now, but getting married is definitely not one of them.

She glances at the pews as she walks past; little bouquets of flowers, tied off with silk ribbons, are balanced on the end of each one. The candles at the front of the church make everything look slightly magical, and the sophistication of the whole thing, the stylish elegance of it, is in such stark contrast to Dad's old life that Hadley's honestly not sure whether to be confused or insulted.

It occurs to her that Charlotte must now be somewhere behind her, waiting in the wings, and the urge to turn around and look nearly overwhelms her. She glances up again, and this time, it's to find Dad's eyes fixed on her. Without really even meaning to, she looks away, using all her concentration to keep herself moving forward, though every part of her is itching to bolt in the opposite direction.

At the top of the aisle, as she and Monty part ways, Dad reaches out and takes Hadley's hand, giving it a little squeeze. The way he looks right now, so tall and handsome in a tux, reminds her of the photos she's seen from when he married Mom, and she swallows hard and manages a small smile before moving to join the rest of the bridesmaids on the other side of the altar. Her eyes travel to the back of the church, and when the music shifts and swells, the guests rise to their feet, and the bride appears in the doorway on the arm of her father.

Hadley had been so prepared to hate Charlotte that she's momentarily stunned by how beautiful she looks in the bell-shaped dress and delicate veil. She's tall and willowy, so different from Mom, who is short and compact, tiny enough that whenever they used to go out Dad would jokingly sweep her up and pretend that he was planning on tossing her into a garbage can.

But now, here in front of her is Charlotte, looking so lovely and graceful that Hadley worries she won't have anything terrible to report to Mom later. Her walk to the front of the church seems endless, yet nobody can look away. And when she finally reaches the altar, her eyes still locked on Dad's, she glances over her shoulder and flashes a smile at a dazed Hadley, who—despite everything, despite all her vows to hate her—grins back reflexively.

And the rest of it? It's the same as it's always been, the same as it always will be. It's identical to a hundred thousand weddings past and a hundred thousand weddings to come. The minister steps up to the altar and the father gives away his daughter with just two simple words. There are prayers delivered and vows recited, and finally there are rings exchanged, too. There are smiles and tears, music and applause, even laughter when the groom messes up, saying "Yes" instead of "I do."

And though all grooms look happy on their wedding day, there's something in the eyes of this one in particular that nearly takes Hadley's breath away. It knocks the wind out of her, that look of his, the joy in his eyes, the depth of his smile. It stops her cold, splits her right open, wrings her heart out like it's nothing more than a wet towel.

It makes her want to go home all over again.

9

Once upon a time, a million years ago, when Hadley was little and her family was still whole, there was a summer evening like any other, with all three of them out in the front
yard. The light was long gone and the crickets were loud
all around them, and Mom and Dad sat on the porch steps
with their shoulders touching, laughing as they watched
Hadley chase fireflies into the darkest corners of the yard.

Each time she got close, the brilliant yellow lights would
disappear again, and so when she finally managed to catch
one, it seemed almost a miracle, like a jewel in her hand.
She cupped it carefully as she walked back to the porch.

"Can I have the bug house?" she asked, and Mom
reached behind her for the jelly jar. They'd made holes in

the lid earlier, so it was now pocked with little openings no bigger than the stars above, and the firefly winked madly through the filmy glass, its wings beating hard. Hadley pressed her face close to examine it.

"It's definitely a good one," Dad said matter-of-factly, and Mom nodded in agreement.

"How come they're called lightning bugs if there's no lightning?" Hadley asked, squinting at it. "Shouldn't they just be called light bugs?"

"Well," Dad said with a grin, "why are ladybugs called ladybugs if they're not all ladies?"

Mom rolled her eyes and Hadley giggled as they all watched the little bug thrash against the thick walls of the jar.

"You remember when we went fishing last summer?" Mom asked later, when they were nearly ready to head in for the night. She snagged the back of Hadley's shirt and tugged gently, walking her back a few steps so that she was half sitting on her lap. "And we threw back all the fish we caught?"

"So they could swim away again."

"Exactly," Mom said, resting her chin on Hadley's shoulder. "I think this guy would be happier, too, if you let him go."

Hadley said nothing, though she hugged the jar a bit closer to her.

"You know what they say," Dad said. "If you love something, set it free."

"What if he doesn't come back?"

"Some things do, some things don't," he said, reaching over to tweak her nose. "*I'll* always come back to you anyway."

"You don't light up," Hadley pointed out, but Dad only smiled.

"I do when I'm with you."

By the time the ceremony is over, the rain has mostly stopped. Even so, there's an impressive flock of black umbrellas outside, guarding against the lingering mist and making the churchyard look more like a funeral gathering than a wedding. From above, the bells are ringing so loudly that Hadley can feel the vibrations straight through to her toes as she makes her way down the steps.

As soon as they'd been pronounced man and wife, Dad and Charlotte had marched triumphantly back up the aisle, where they'd promptly disappeared. Even now, a full fifteen minutes after they sealed the deal with a kiss, Hadley hasn't seen any sign of them. She wanders aimlessly through the crowd, wondering how Dad could possibly know this many people. He lived in Connecticut for nearly his whole life and has only a few token friends to show for it. A couple years over here, and he's apparently some kind of social butterfly.

Besides which, most of the guests look like extras from a

movie set, plucked straight out of someone else's life entirely. Since when does her father hang out with women in fancy hats and men in morning suits, all of them dressed as if they've dropped by on their way to tea with the Queen? The whole scene—combined with her mounting jet lag—makes Hadley feel not quite awake, like she's a beat or two behind the present moment and trying unsuccessfully to catch up.

As a sliver of sun breaks through the clouds, the wedding guests tilt their heads back and lower their umbrellas, marveling as if they're fortunate enough to be bearing witness to the rarest of weather anomalies. Standing in their midst, Hadley isn't quite sure what's required of her at the moment. The other bridesmaids don't appear to be around, and it's entirely possible she's meant to be doing something more useful right now; she didn't exactly read all of the schedules and directions that had been e-mailed to her over the past few weeks, and there'd been no time to get further instruction before the ceremony.

"Am I supposed to be somewhere?" she asks when she stumbles across Monty, who's circling the vintage white limousine out front with great interest. He shrugs, then immediately resumes his inspection of the car that will presumably whisk the happy couple off to the reception later.

On her way back toward the church entrance, Hadley is relieved to spot a purple dress in the crowd, which turns out to be Violet.

"Your dad's looking for you," Violet says, pointing at the old stone building. "He and Charlotte are inside. She's just getting her makeup retouched a bit before it's time for photos."

"When's the reception?" Hadley asks, and the way Violet looks at her, it's as if she's inquired as to where the sky's located. Apparently, this is a rather obvious piece of information.

"Did you not get an itinerary?"

"I didn't get a chance to look at it," Hadley says sheepishly.

"It's not till six."

"So what do we do between now and then?"

"Well, the photos will take a while."

"And then?"

Violet shrugs. "Everyone's staying at the hotel."

Hadley gives her a blank look.

"Which is where the reception is," she explains. "So I suppose we'll probably go back there in between."

"Fun," Hadley says, and Violet raises an eyebrow.

"Aren't you going to go find your dad?"

"Right," she says without moving. "Yup."

"He's in the church," Violet repeats, forming the words slowly, as if worried that her friend's new stepdaughter might be a few ants shy of a picnic. "Right over there."

When Hadley still makes no sort of overture to leave, Violet's face softens.

"Look," she says, "my father remarried when I was a bit

younger than you are. So I get it. But you could do a lot worse than Charlotte as a stepmum, you know?"

In fact, Hadley doesn't know. She barely knows anything about Charlotte at all, but she doesn't say this.

Violet frowns. "I thought mine was really awful. I hated her for asking me to do even the smallest things, things my own mum would have made me do, too, like going to church or doing chores around the house. With stuff like that, it's just a matter of who's doing the asking, and because it was her, I hated it." She pauses, smiling. "Then one day, I realized it wasn't her that I was really angry with. It was him."

Hadley looks off toward the church for a moment before answering. "Then I guess," she says finally, "that I'm already a step ahead of you."

Violet nods, perhaps realizing that there's not much progress to be made on the subject, and gives Hadley's shoulder an awkward little pat. As she turns to leave, Hadley is filled with a sudden dread for whatever it is that awaits her inside the church. What exactly are you supposed to say to the father you haven't seen in ages on the occasion of his wedding to a woman you've never met? If there's an appropriate etiquette for this sort of situation, she's certainly not familiar with it.

Inside, the church is quiet. Everyone is outside waiting for the bride and groom to emerge. Her heels echo loudly on the tiled floors as she wanders toward the basement, trailing a hand along the rough stone walls. Near the stairs, the sound of voices drifts upward like smoke, and Hadley pauses at the top to listen.

"You don't mind, then?" a woman asks, and another one murmurs something that's too soft for Hadley to hear. "I'd think it'd make things tough."

"Not at all," says the other woman, and Hadley realizes that it's Charlotte. "Besides, she lives with her mum."

From where she's standing, frozen at the top of the stairs, Hadley catches her breath.

Here it comes, she thinks. *The wicked stepmother moment.*

Here's the part where she overhears all the awful things they've been saying about her, where she discovers how glad they are that she's out of the picture, that she's not wanted anyway. She's spent so many months imagining this, picturing just how awful Charlotte might be, and now that the moment is finally here, she's so busy waiting for the proof that she nearly misses the next part.

"I'd like to get to know her better," Charlotte is saying. "I really do hope they patch things up soon."

The other woman lets out a soft laugh. "Like in the next nine months?"

"Well..." Charlotte says, and Hadley can hear the smile in her voice. It's enough to send her backward several steps, stumbling a bit in her too-high heels. The empty halls of the church are dark and silent, and she feels suddenly chilled despite the temperature.

Nine months, she thinks, her eyes pricking with tears.

Her first thought is for her mother, though whether it's a

wish to protect or to *be* protected, she's not really sure. Either way, she wants nothing more than to hear her mom's voice right now. But her phone is downstairs, in the same room as Charlotte, and besides, how could she be the one to break the news? She knows Mom has a tendency to take these things in stride, always as wholly unruffled as Hadley is irrational. But this is different. This is huge. And it seems impossible that even Mom could avoid feeling rattled by this piece of news.

Hadley certainly is, anyway.

She's still perched there like that, leaning against the doorframe and glaring at the stairs, when she hears footsteps around the corner, and the deep sound of men laughing. She darts down the hall a little ways so that it won't look as if she's been doing precisely what she's been doing, and is there examining her fingernails with what she hopes is a look of great nonchalance when Dad appears alongside the minister.

"Hadley," he says, clapping a hand on her shoulder and addressing her as if they see each other every day. "I want you to meet Reverend Walker."

"Nice to meet you, dear," the elderly man says, taking her hand and then turning back to Dad. "I'll see you at the reception, Andrew. Congratulations again."

"Thanks so much, Reverend," he says, and then the two of them are left there to watch as the minister hobbles off again, his black robes trailing behind him like a cape.

When he's disappeared around the corner, Dad turns back to Hadley with a grin.

"It's good to see you, kiddo," he says, and Hadley feels her smile wobble and then fall. She glances over at the basement door, and those two words go skidding through her head again.

Nine months.

Dad is standing close enough that she can smell his aftershave, minty and sharp, and the rush of memories it brings makes her heart quicken. He's looking at her like he's waiting for something—for what?—as if she should be the one to begin this charade, crack open her heart and spill it right there at his feet.

As if she's the one with secrets to tell.

She's spent so much time avoiding him, so much effort trying to cut him out of her life—as if it were that easy, as if he were as insubstantial as a paper doll—and now it turns out *he's* the one who's been keeping something from *her*.

"Congrats," Hadley croaks, submitting to a somewhat stilted hug, which ends up as more of a pat on the back than anything else.

Dad steps away awkwardly. "I'm glad you made it."

"Me, too," she says. "It was nice."

"Charlotte's excited to meet you," he says, and Hadley bristles.

"Great," she manages to say.

Dad gives her a hopeful smile. "I think you two will get on brilliantly."

"Great," she says again.

He clears his throat and fidgets with his bow tie, looking

stiff and uncomfortable, though whether it's the tux or the situation, Hadley isn't sure.

"Listen," he says. "I'm actually glad I found you alone. There's something I want to talk to you about."

Hadley stands up a bit straighter, steeling herself as if to absorb a great impact. She doesn't have time to be relieved that he's actually going to tell her after all; she's so busy working out how to react to the news of the baby—sullen silence? fake surprise? shocked disbelief?—that her face is wiped clean as a chalkboard when he finally delivers the blow.

"Charlotte was really hoping we'd do a father-daughter dance at the reception," he says, and Hadley—somehow more stunned by this than by the far more shattering news she'd been prepared for—simply stares at him.

Dad holds up his hands. "I know, I know," he says. "I told her you'd hate it, that there's no way you'd want to be out there in front of everyone with your old man...." He trails off, obviously waiting for Hadley to jump in.

"I'm not much of a dancer," she says eventually.

"I know," he says, grinning. "Neither am I. But it's Charlotte's day, and it seems really important to her, and..."

"Fine," Hadley says, blinking hard.

"Fine?"

"Fine."

"Well, great," he says, sounding genuinely surprised. He rocks back on his heels, beaming at this unexpected victory. "Charlotte will be thrilled."

"I'm glad," Hadley says, unable to hide the note of bitterness in her voice. All of a sudden she feels hollowed out, no longer in the mood to fight. She asked for this, after all. She wanted nothing to do with his new life, and now here he is, starting it without her.

But it isn't just about Charlotte anymore. In nine months, he'll have a new baby, too, maybe even another daughter.

And he hadn't even bothered to tell her.

She's stung by this in the same place that had been hurt by his leaving, the same tender spot that had ached when she'd first heard about Charlotte. But this time, almost without realizing, Hadley finds herself leaning into it rather than away.

After all, it's one thing to run away when someone's chasing you.

It's entirely another to be running all alone.

10

Late last night, as she and Oliver had shared a pack of tiny pretzels on the plane, he'd been quiet, studying her profile for so long without speaking that she'd finally turned to face him.

"What?"

"What do you want to be when you grow up?"

She frowned. "That's a question you ask a four-year-old."

"Not necessarily," he said. "Everyone has to be something."

"What do *you* want to be?"

He shrugged. "I asked you first."

"An astronaut," she said. "A ballerina."

"Seriously."

"You don't think I could be an astronaut?"

"You could be the first ballerina on the moon."

"I guess I've still got some time to figure it out."

"That's true," he said.

"And you?" she asked, expecting another sarcastic answer, some invented profession having to do with his mysterious research project.

"I don't know, either," he said quietly. "Certainly not a lawyer, anyway."

Hadley raised her eyebrows. "Is that what your dad does?"

But he didn't answer; he only glared harder at the pretzel in his hand. "Never mind all this," he said after a moment. "Who wants to think about the future, anyway?"

"Not me," she said. "I can hardly stand to think of the next few hours, much less the next few years."

"That's why flying's so great," he said. "You're stuck where you are. You've got no choice in the matter."

Hadley smiled at him. "It's not the worst place to be stuck."

"No, it's not," Oliver agreed, popping the last pretzel in his mouth. "In fact, there's nowhere else I'd rather be right now."

In the hallway of the darkened church Dad paces restlessly, checking his watch and craning his neck toward the stairs every now and then as they wait for Charlotte to emerge from the basement. He looks like a teenager, flushed and eager for his date to arrive, and the thought crosses Hadley's mind that maybe this is what *he* wanted to be when he grew up. Husband to Charlotte. Father to her baby. A man who spends Christmas in Scotland and goes on holiday to the south of France, who talks about art and politics and literature over slow-cooked meals and bottles of wine.

How odd that things turned out this way, especially since he'd been so close to staying home. Dream job or not, four months had seemed like such a long time to be away, and if it hadn't been for Mom—who urged him to go, who said it was his dream, who insisted he'd regret passing up such an opportunity—Dad would never even have met Charlotte in the first place.

But here they are, and as if cued by Hadley's unspoken musings, Charlotte appears at the top of the stairs, pink-cheeked and radiant in her dress. Without the veil, her auburn hair now hangs in loose curls to her shoulders, and she seems to glide right into Dad's arms. Hadley looks away when they kiss, shifting uncomfortably from one foot to the other. After a moment, Dad breaks away and sweeps an arm in Hadley's direction.

"I'd like you to meet my daughter," he says to Charlotte. "Officially."

Charlotte beams at her. "I'm so pleased you could make it," she says, pulling Hadley into a hug. She smells of lilacs, though it's hard to tell whether it's her perfume or the bouquet she's holding. Taking a step back again, Hadley notices the ring on her finger, at least double the size of Mom's, which Hadley still sneaks out of the jewelry box from time to time, slipping it onto her thumb and examining the carved faces of the diamond as if they might hold the key to her parents' unraveling.

"Sorry it took me so long," Charlotte says, turning back to Dad. "But you only get to take your wedding photos once."

Hadley considers mentioning that this is in fact Dad's second time around, but she manages to bite her tongue.

"Don't listen to her," Dad says to Hadley. "She takes this long even when she's just going out to the market."

Charlotte whacks him lightly with her bouquet. "Aren't you supposed to act like a gentleman on your wedding day?"

Dad leans in and gives her a quick kiss. "For you, I'll try."

Hadley flicks her eyes away again, feeling like an intruder. She wishes she could slip outside without their noticing, but Charlotte is now smiling at her again with an expression Hadley isn't quite sure how to read.

"Has your dad had a chance to tell you about—"

"The father-daughter dance?" Dad says, cutting her off. "Yeah, I told her."

"Brilliant," Charlotte says, putting an arm around Hadley's shoulders conspiratorially. "I've already made sure there'll be plenty of ice at the reception for when your dad steps all over our toes."

Hadley smiles weakly. "Great."

"We should probably get out there and say a quick hello to everyone before it's time for photos," Dad suggests. "And then the whole wedding party is going back to the hotel before the reception," he tells Hadley. "So we just need to remember to grab your suitcase before we head over."

"Sure," she says, allowing herself to be led in the direction of the open doors at the end of the long corridor. She feels a bit like she's sleepwalking and concentrates on putting one foot in front of the other, figuring the only way out of this—this wedding, this weekend, this whole blessed event—is to just keep moving forward.

"Hey," Dad says, pausing just before they reach the door. He leans over and kisses Hadley's forehead. "I'm really glad you're here."

"Me, too," she murmurs, falling back again as Dad loops an arm around Charlotte, pulling her close before they step outside together. A cheer goes up from the crowd at the sight of them, and though she knows all eyes are on the bride, Hadley still feels far too visible, so she hangs back until Dad half turns and motions for her to follow them.

The sky above is still shot through with silver, a glittery mix of sun and clouds, and the umbrellas have all but disappeared. Hadley trails after the happy couple as Dad shakes hands and Charlotte kisses cheeks, occasionally introducing her to people she'll never remember, repeating names she barely hears—Dad's colleague Justin and Charlotte's wayward cousin Carrie; the flower girls, Aishling and Niamh; and Reverend Walker's portly wife—the whole unfamiliar cast assembled on the lawn like a reminder of all that Hadley doesn't know about her father.

It seems that most of the guests will attend the reception later this evening, but they're unable to wait until then to offer their heartfelt congratulations, and the joy in their faces is contagious. Even Hadley can't help but be stirred by the momentousness of the day, until she notices a woman balancing a baby on her hip, and the leaden feeling returns again.

"Hadley," Dad is saying as he guides her over to an older couple, "I want you to meet some very good friends of Charlotte's family, the O'Callaghans."

Hadley shakes each of their hands, nodding politely. "Nice to meet you."

"So this is the famous Hadley," says Mr. O'Callaghan. "We've heard so much about you."

It's difficult to hide her surprise. "Really?"

"Of course," Dad says, squeezing her shoulder. "How many daughters do you think I have?"

Hadley is still just staring at him, unsure of what to say, when Charlotte arrives at his side again and greets the older couple warmly.

"We just wanted to say congratulations before we go," says Mrs. O'Callaghan. "We've got a funeral, of all things, but we'll be back for the reception later."

"Oh, how sad," Charlotte says. "I'm so sorry. Whose is it?"

"An old friend of Tom's, from his Oxford law days."

"That's terrible," Dad says. "Is it far?"

"Paddington," Mr. O'Callaghan says, and Hadley whips her head to look at him.

"Paddington?"

He nods, looking at her a little uncertainly, then turns back to Dad and Charlotte. "It starts at two, so we'd better be off. But congrats again," he says. "We're looking forward to tonight."

As they leave, Hadley stares after them, her mind racing. The thinnest sliver of a thought is threading its way through her, but before she has a chance to grab hold of it Violet pushes through the crowd to announce that it's time for photos.

"Hope you're ready to smile till your face hurts," she tells Hadley, who is about as far from ready to smile as is possible right now. Once again, she allows herself to be nudged forward, malleable as a piece of putty, as Dad and Charlotte follow along behind her, leaning into each other as if there's nobody else around.

"Ah, I *thought* we were missing somebody," jokes the photographer when she sees the bride and groom. The rest of the wedding party is already gathered in the garden around the side of the church, the same place where Hadley found her way inside earlier. One of the other bridesmaids hands her a small mirror, and she holds it gingerly, blinking back at herself, her mind a million miles away.

Hadley has no idea whether Paddington is a town or a neighborhood or even just a street. All she knows is that it's where Oliver lives, and she squeezes her eyes shut and tries to think back to what he said on the plane. Someone takes the mirror from her clammy hands, and she blindly follows the photographer's pointed finger to a spot on the grass, where she stands obediently as the others assemble themselves around her.

When she's told to smile, Hadley forces her lips into a shape that she hopes might resemble one. But her eyes sting with the effort of organizing her thoughts, and all she can picture is Oliver at the airport with that suit slung over his shoulder.

Had he ever actually said he was going to a wedding?

The camera clicks and whirs as the photographer arranges the wedding party in different combinations: the whole group; then just the women and just the men; then several variations on the family itself, the most awkward of which involves Hadley standing between her father and her brand-new stepmother. It's impossible to know how she gets from one spot to another, but somehow she's there all the same, her smile so falsely bright that her cheeks ache, her heart sinking like a weight in water.

It's him, she thinks as the camera flashes. *It's Oliver's father.*

She knows nothing for sure, of course, but as soon as she attaches the words to it, gives name to the shapeless thoughts in her head, she's suddenly certain it must be true.

"Dad," she says quietly, and from where he's standing beside her, he moves his head just the tiniest bit, his smile unchanging.

"Yeah?" he asks through his teeth.

Charlotte's eyes slide over in Hadley's direction, then back to the camera.

"I have to go."

Dad looks over at her this time and the photographer straightens with a frown and says, "You'll have to stay still."

"Just a minute," he tells her, holding up a finger. To Hadley, he says, "Go where?"

Everyone is looking at her now: the florist, who's trying to keep the bouquets from wilting; the rest of the brides-maids, observing the family shoot from the sidelines; the photographer's assistant, with her clipboard. Someone's baby lets out a sharp cry, and from atop the statue the pigeons take flight. Everyone is looking, but Hadley doesn't care. Because the possibility that Oliver—who spent half the flight listening to her complain about this wedding like it was a tragedy of epic proportions—might be preparing for his father's funeral at this very moment is almost too much to bear.

Nobody here will understand; she knows that much is true. She's not even sure she understands herself. Yet there's an urgency to the decision, a kind of slow and desperate momentum. Each time she closes her eyes, he's there again: Oliver telling her the story of the night-light, his eyes distant and his voice hollow.

"It's just..." she begins, then trails off again. "There's something I need to do."

Dad raises both hands and looks around, clearly unable

141

to fathom what this might be. *"Now?"* he asks, his voice tight. "What could you possibly have to do at this exact moment? In *London?"*

Charlotte is watching them, her mouth open.

"Please, Dad," she says, her voice soft. "It's important."

He shakes his head. "I don't think…"

But she's already backing away. "I swear I'll be back for the reception," she says. "And I'll have my phone."

"Where are you even *going?"*

"I'll be fine," she says, still moving backward, though this is clearly not the answer her dad was looking for. She gives a little wave as she reaches the door to the church. Everyone is still eyeing her as if she's lost her mind, and maybe she has, but she needs to know for sure. She grabs the handle and braves one last glance back at Dad, who looks furious. His hands are on his hips, his forehead creased. She waves again and then steps inside, letting the door close behind her.

The stillness of the church comes as a shock, and Hadley stands there with her back against the cool stone of the wall, waiting for someone—Dad or Charlotte, the wedding planner or a posse of bridesmaids—to come after her. But nobody does, and she suspects this isn't because Dad understands. How could he? It's far more likely that he just doesn't remember how to be this kind of parent anymore. It's one thing to be the guy who calls on Christmas; it's another to have to discipline your teenage daughter in front of everyone you know, especially when you're no longer quite sure of the rules.

Hadley feels guilty for taking advantage of him like this, especially on his wedding day, but it's like the lens has shifted; her focus is now clear.

All she wants is to get to Oliver.

Downstairs, she hurries to the classroom where she left her bags. As she walks past the mirror she catches a glimpse of herself, looking young and pale and so very uncertain, and she feels her resolve start to crumble. Maybe she's jumping to conclusions. Maybe she's wrong about Oliver's dad. She has no idea where she's going, and there's a good possibility that her own father won't ever forgive her for this.

But when she reaches for her purse the napkin with Oliver's drawing flutters to the floor, and she finds herself smiling as she stoops to pick it up, running her thumb across the little duck with sneakers and a baseball cap.

Maybe this *is* a mistake.

But there's still no place else she'd rather be right now.

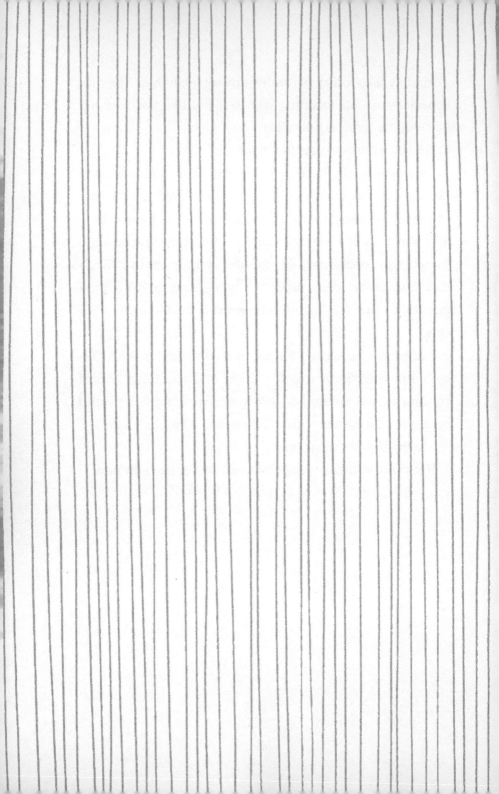

11

9:00 AM Eastern Standard Time
2:00 PM Greenwich Mean Time

Hadley is already out the door and across the street, the church bells tolling two o'clock in her wake, before she realizes she has no idea where she's going. An enormous red bus races past and, surprised, she stumbles backward a few steps before taking off after it. Even without her suitcase—which she left in the church—she's still too slow, and by the time she makes it around the corner, the bus has already pulled away again.

Panting, she stoops to squint at the bus map that's plastered at the stop behind a thick pane of glass, though it turns out to be little more than a mystifying tangle of colored lines and unfamiliar names. She bites her lip as she studies it, thinking there must be a better way to crack this code, when she finally spots Paddington in the upper left-hand corner.

It doesn't look all that far, but then, it's hard to get a feel for the scale of the thing, and for all Hadley knows, it's just as likely to be miles away as blocks. There's not enough detail to pick out any landmarks, and she still has no clue what she'll do once she gets there; the only thing she remembers Oliver saying about the church is that there's a statue of Mary out front and that he and his brothers used to get in trouble for climbing it. She glances at the map again. How many churches could there be in such a small patch of London? How many statues?

No matter the distance, she has only ten pounds in her purse, and judging by the cab ride from the airport, that will barely get her from here to the mailbox at the corner. The stubborn map still refuses to give up its secrets, so she decides it's probably easiest to just ask the driver of the next bus that comes along and hope he'll be able to point her in the right direction. But after nearly ten minutes of waiting with no sign of a bus, she takes another stab at deciphering the routes, tapping her fingers on the glass with obvious impatience.

"You know the saying, don't you?" says a man in a soccer jersey. Hadley straightens up, acutely aware of how overdressed she is for a bus ride through London. When she doesn't respond, the guy continues. "You wait for ages, and then two come along at once."

"Am I in the right place to get to Paddington?"

"Paddington?" he says. "Yeah, you're grand."

When the bus arrives the man smiles encouragingly, so Hadley doesn't bother asking the driver. But as she watches out the window for signs, she wonders how she'll know when they've arrived, since most stops are labeled by street name rather than area. After a good fifteen minutes of aimless sightseeing, she finally works up the nerve to teeter to the front of the bus and ask which stop is hers.

"Paddington?" the driver says, showing a gold tooth as he grins. "You're headed in the wrong bloody direction."

Hadley groans. "Can you tell me which way is the *right* bloody direction?"

He lets her off near Westminster with directions for how to get to Paddington by tube, and she pauses for a moment on the sidewalk. Her eyes travel up to the sky, where she's surprised to see a plane flying overhead, and something about the sight of it calms her again. She's suddenly back in seat 18A beside Oliver, suspended above the water, surrounded by nothing but darkness.

And there on the street corner, it strikes her as something of a miracle that she met him at all. Imagine if she'd been on time for her flight. Or if she'd spent all those hours beside someone else, a complete stranger who, even after so many miles, remained that way. The idea that their paths might have just as easily *not* crossed leaves her breathless, like a near-miss accident on a highway, and she can't help marveling at the sheer randomness of it all. Like any survivor of chance, she feels a quick rush of thankfulness, part adrenaline and part hope.

She picks her way through the crowded London streets, keeping an eye out for the tube stop. The city is crooked and twisty, full of curved avenues and winding alleys, like some kind of grand Victorian maze. It's a beautiful summer Saturday and people fill the sidewalks, carrying bags from the market, pushing strollers, walking dogs, and jogging toward the parks. She passes a boy wearing the same blue shirt Oliver had on earlier and her heart quickens at the sight of it.

For the first time, Hadley regrets not having visited her dad here, if only for this: the aging buildings, so full of character, the roadside stalls, the red telephone booths and black taxis and stone churches. Everything in this city seems old, but charmingly so, like something out of a movie, and if she weren't racing from a wedding to a funeral and back again, if she weren't wound quite so tightly at the moment, if every bone in her body weren't aching to see Oliver, she thinks she might even like to spend some time here.

When she finally spots the red and blue sign for the tube she hurries down the stairs, blinking into the darkness of the underground. It takes her too long to figure out the ticket machines, and she can feel the people in line behind her shifting restlessly. Finally, a woman who looks a bit like the Queen takes pity on her, first telling her which options to choose, then nudging Hadley aside to do it herself.

"Here you go, love," she says, handing over the ticket. "Enjoy your trip."

The bus driver told Hadley she'd probably need to switch trains at some point, but as far as she can tell from the map, she can get there directly on the Circle Line. There's a digital sign that says the tube will arrive in six minutes, so she presses herself into a small wedge of open space on the platform to wait.

Her eyes travel over the advertisements on the walls as she listens to the accents all around her, not just British but French and Italian and others she doesn't even recognize. There's a policeman standing nearby wearing a sort of old-fashioned helmet, and a man tossing a soccer ball from one hand to the other. When a little girl begins to cry, her mother bends at the waist and shushes her in another language, something guttural and harsh. The girl bursts into tears all over again.

Nobody is looking at Hadley, not one person, but even so, she's never felt more visible in her life: too small, too American, too obviously alone and unsure of herself.

She doesn't want to think about Dad and the wedding she left behind, and she's not sure she wants to think about Oliver and what she might discover when she finds him. The train is still four minutes away and her head is pounding. The silky fabric of her dress feels far too sticky and the woman beside her is standing much too close. Hadley scrunches her nose against the smell of the place, musty and stale and sour all at once, like fruit gone bad in a small space.

She closes her eyes and thinks of her father's advice to

her when they stood in the elevator in Aspen, the walls collapsing like a house of cards all around her, and she imagines the sky beyond the arched ceiling of the tube stop, above the sidewalk and past the narrow buildings. There's a pattern to this kind of coping, like a dream repeated night after night, always the same image: a few wispy clouds like a streak of paint across a blue canvas. But now she's surprised to find something new in the picture that's forming on the backs of her eyelids, something cutting across the blue sky of her imagination: an airplane.

Her eyes flicker open again as the train comes rushing out of the tunnel.

Hadley's never sure if things are as small as they seem, or if it's just her panic that seems to dwarf them. When she thinks back, she often remembers stadiums as little more than gymnasiums; sprawling houses become apartment-sized in her mind because of the sheer number of people packed in. So it's hard to tell for sure whether the tube is actually smaller than the subway cars back home, which she's ridden a thousand times with a kind of tentative calm, or whether it's the knot in her chest that makes it seem like a matchbox car.

Much to her relief, she finds a seat on the end of a row, then immediately closes her eyes again. But it's not working, and as the train lurches out of the station she remembers the book in her bag and pulls it out, grateful for the distraction. She brushes her thumb across the words on the cover before opening it.

When she was little, Hadley used to sneak into Dad's office at home, which was lined with bookshelves that stretched from the floor to the ceiling, all of them stacked with peeling paperbacks and hardcovers with cracked spines. She was only six the first time he found her sitting in his armchair with her stuffed elephant and a copy of *A Christmas Carol,* poring over it as intently as if she were considering it for her dissertation.

"What're you reading?" he'd asked, leaning against the doorframe and taking off his glasses.

"A story."

"Yeah?" he asked, trying not to smile. "What story?"

"It's about a girl and her elephant," Hadley informed him matter-of-factly.

"Is that right?"

"Yes," she said. "And they go on a trip together, on a bike, but then the elephant runs away, and she cries so hard that someone brings her a flower."

Dad crossed the room and in a single practiced motion lifted her from the chair—Hadley clinging desperately to the slender book—until, suddenly, she was sitting on his lap.

"What happens next?" he asked.

"The elephant finds her again."

"And then?"

"He gets a cupcake. And they live happily ever after."

"That sounds like a great story."

Hadley squeezed the fraying elephant on her lap. "It was."

"Do you want me to read you another one?" he asked,

gently taking the book from her and flipping to the first page. "It's about Christmas."

She settled back into the soft flannel of his shirt, and he began to read.

It wasn't even the story itself that she loved; she didn't understand half the words and often felt lost in the winding sentences. It was the gruff sound of her father's voice, the funny accents he did for each character, the way he let her turn the pages. Every night after dinner they would read together in the stillness of the study. Sometimes Mom would come stand at the door with a dish towel in her hand and a half-smile on her face as she listened, but mostly it was just the two of them.

Even when she was old enough to read herself, they still tackled the classics together, moving from *Anna Karenina* to *Pride and Prejudice* to *The Grapes of Wrath* as if traveling across the globe itself, leaving holes in the bookshelves like missing teeth.

And later, when it started to become clear that she cared more about soccer practice and phone privileges than Jane Austen or Walt Whitman, when the hour turned into a half hour and every night turned into every other, it no longer mattered. The stories had become a part of her by then; they stuck to her bones like a good meal, bloomed inside of her like a garden. They were as deep and meaningful as any other trait Dad had passed along to her: her blue eyes, her straw-colored hair, the sprinkling of freckles across her nose.

Often he would come home with books for her, for Christmas or her birthday, or for no particular occasion at all, some of them early editions with beautiful gold trim, others used paperbacks bought for a dollar or two on a street corner. Mom always looked exasperated, especially when it was a new copy of one that he already had in his study.

"This house is about two dictionaries away from caving in," she'd say, "and you're buying duplicates?"

But Hadley understood. It wasn't that she was meant to read them all. Maybe someday she would, but for now, it was more the gesture itself. He was giving her the most important thing he could, the only way he knew how. He was a professor, a lover of stories, and he was building her a library in the same way other men might build their daughters houses.

So when he'd given her the worn copy of *Our Mutual Friend* that day in Aspen, after everything that had happened, there was something too familiar in the gesture. She'd been rubbed raw by his departure, and the meaning behind the gift made it hurt all the more. And so Hadley had done what she did best: She simply ignored it.

But now, as the train snakes its way beneath the streets of London, she's unexpectedly pleased to have it. It's been years since she's read anything by Dickens; first, because there were other things to do, better things to do, and then later, she supposed, because she was making some sort of quiet statement against her dad.

People talk about books being an escape, but here on the

tube, this one feels more like a lifeline. As she leafs through the pages, the rest of it fades away: the flurry of elbows and purses, the woman in a tunic biting her fingernails, the two teenagers with blaring headphones, even the man playing the violin at the other end of the car, its reedy tune working its way through the crowd. The motion of the train makes her head rattle, but her eyes lock on the words the way a figure skater might choose a focal point as she spins, and just like that, she's grounded again.

As she skips from one chapter to the next, Hadley forgets that she ever meant to return the book. The words, of course, are not her father's, but he's there in the pages all the same, and the reminder kick-starts something inside her.

Just before her stop she pauses, trying to recall the underlined sentence she'd discovered on the plane earlier. As she thumbs through the book, her eyes skimming for any sign of ink, she's surprised to find another one.

"And O there are days in this life, worth life and worth death," it reads, and Hadley lifts her gaze, feeling a hitch in her chest.

Only this morning the wedding had seemed the worst possible thing in the world, but now she understands that there are far grimmer ceremonies, far worse things that can happen on any given day. And as she exits the train along with the other passengers, past the words PADDING-TON STATION, spelled out in tiles along the wall, she only hopes she's wrong about what she might discover here.

12

Outside, the sun has come out of hiding, though the streets are still damp and silvery. Hadley spins in a circle, trying to get her bearings, taking in the white-trimmed pharmacy, the little antique shop, the rows of pale-colored buildings stretching the length of the road. A group of men in rugby shirts emerge bleary-eyed from a pub, and a few women with shopping bags brush past her on the sidewalk.

Hadley glances at her watch; nearly three PM, and she has no idea what to do now that she's here. As far as she can tell, there are no policemen around, no tourist offices or information booths, no bookstores or Internet cafés. It's like she's been dropped into the wilderness of London without a compass or a map, like some sort of ill-conceived challenge on a reality show.

She picks a direction at random and sets off down the street, wishing she'd stopped to change her shoes before bailing on the wedding. There's a fish 'n' chips place on the corner, and her stomach rumbles at the smells drifting from the door; the last thing she ate was that pack of pretzels on the plane, and the last time she slept was just before that. She'd like nothing more than to curl up and take a nap right now, but she keeps moving anyway, fueled by a strange mix of fear and longing.

After ten minutes and two emerging blisters, she still hasn't passed a church. She ducks into a bookshop to ask if anybody knows about a statue of Mary, but the man looks at her so strangely that she backs out again without waiting for an answer.

Along the narrow sidewalks are butcher shops with huge cuts of meat hanging in the windows, clothing stores with mannequins in heels much higher than Hadley's, pubs and restaurants, even a library that she nearly mistakes for a chapel. But as she circles the neighborhood, there doesn't seem to be a single church in sight, not one bell tower or steeple, until — quite suddenly — there is.

Emerging from an alleyway, she spots a narrow stone building across the street. She hesitates a moment, blinking at it like a mirage, then rushes forward, buoyed again. But then the bells begin to ring in a way that seems far too joyful for the occasion, and a wedding party spills out onto the steps.

Hadley hadn't realized she was holding her breath, but it comes rushing out of her now. She waits for the taxis to stop hurrying past and then crosses the street to confirm what she already knows: no funeral, no statue of Mary, no Oliver.

Even so, she can't seem to pull herself away, and she stands there watching the aftermath of a wedding not unlike the one she just witnessed herself, the flower girls and the bridesmaids, the flashes of the cameras, the friends and family all wreathed in smiles. The bells finish their merry song and the sun slips lower in the sky and still she just stands there. After a long moment, she reaches into her purse. Then she does what she always does when she's lost: She calls her mother.

Her phone is nearly out of battery power, and her fingers tremble as she punches in the numbers, anxious as she is to hear Mom's voice. It seems impossible that the last time they talked they had a fight and, even more, that it happened less than twenty-four hours ago. The departures lane at the airport now seems like something from another lifetime.

They've always been close, she and Mom, but after Dad left, something shifted. Hadley was angry, furious in a way she hadn't known was possible. But Mom—Mom was just broken. For weeks she'd moved as if she were underwater, red-eyed and heavy-footed, coming alive again only when the phone rang, her whole body quivering like a tuning fork as she waited to hear that Dad had changed his mind.

But he never did.

In those weeks after Christmas their roles had flip-flopped; it was Hadley who brought Mom dinner every night, who lay awake with worry as she listened to her cry, who made sure there was always a fresh box of Kleenex on the nightstand.

And this was the most unfair part of it all: What Dad had done, he hadn't just done to him and Mom, and he hadn't just done to him and Hadley. He'd done it to Hadley and Mom, too, had turned the easy rhythms between them into something brittle and complicated, something that could shatter at any moment. It seemed to Hadley that things would never return to normal, that they were forever meant to pinball between anger and grief, the hole in their house big enough to swallow them both.

But then, just like that, it was over.

About a month had passed when Mom appeared at Hadley's bedroom door one morning, decked out in her now familiar uniform of a hooded sweatshirt and a pair of Dad's old flannel pajama pants, much too long and far too big for her.

"Enough of this," she said. "Let's get out of here."

Hadley frowned. "What?"

"Pack your bags, kid," Mom said, sounding almost like herself again. "We're going on a trip."

It was late January, and outside everything was as bleak as it was inside. But by the time they stepped off the plane in Arizona, Hadley could already see something in Mom beginning to unfold, that part of her that had been clenched too tight, that had been curled up in a little ball inside her. They spent a long weekend by the pool at the resort, their skin turning brown and their hair going blonder in the sun. At night they watched movies and ate burgers and played miniature golf, and though she kept waiting for Mom to crumble, to drop the act and melt into a little puddle of tears the way she'd been doing for weeks, it never happened. It occurred to Hadley that if this was how life was going to be from now on—just one long girls' weekend—then maybe it wouldn't be so bad after all.

But it wasn't until they arrived home again that she realized the true purpose of the trip; she could feel it right away, from the moment they walked into the house, like the electricity that lingers after a thunderstorm.

Dad had been there.

The kitchen was cold and dim, and the two of them stood there, silently assessing the damage. It was the little things that stunned Hadley the most, not the obvious absences—the coats on the hooks by the back door, or the wool blanket that was usually draped over the couch in the next room—but the smaller pockets of space: the missing ceramic jar she'd made him in pottery class, the framed photo of his parents that had sat on the hutch, the empty spot in the cabinet where his mug had always been. It was like the scene of a crime, as if the house had been stripped for its parts, and Hadley's first thought was for Mom.

But one look told her that her mother already knew about this.

"Why didn't you tell me?"

Mom was in the living room now, her fingers trailing over the furniture as if she were taking stock of things. "I thought it would be too hard."

"For who?" Hadley asked, her eyes flashing.

Mom didn't answer, only looked at her calmly, with a patience that felt like permission; it was Hadley's turn to be shaken now, Hadley's turn to come undone.

"We thought it would be too hard for you to watch," Mom said. "He wanted to see you, but not like this. Not while he was moving out."

"I'm the one who's been holding it together," Hadley said, her voice small. "*I* should be the one to decide what's too hard."

"Hadley," Mom said softly, taking a step toward her, but Hadley backed away.

"Don't," she said, swallowing back tears. Because it was true; all this time she *had* been the one to hold it together. All this time, she'd been the one to keep them moving forward. But now she could feel herself falling to pieces, and when Mom finally folded her into a hug, all the blurriness of the past month seemed to snap back into focus again, and for the first time since Dad left Hadley felt the anger inside of her loosening, replaced with a sadness so big it was hard to see past it. She pressed her face into Mom's shoulder, and they stood there like that for a long time,

Mom's arms around her as Hadley cried a month's worth of tears.

Six weeks later Hadley would meet Dad in Aspen for their ski trip, and Mom would see her off at the airport with the same measured calm that seemed to have come over her now, an unexpected peace, as fragile as it was certain. Hadley could never be sure whether it was Arizona that did it—the sudden change, the constant sun—or if it was the jarring finality of Dad's missing things upon their return home, but either way, something had changed.

A week later, Hadley's tooth began to ache.

"Too many sweets from the minibar," Mom joked as they drove to the dentist's office that afternoon, Hadley's hand clapped over her jaw.

Their old dentist had retired not long after her last appointment, and the new one was a balding man in his early fifties with a kind face and a starched smock. When he poked his head around the corner of the waiting room to call her in, Hadley saw his eyes widen slightly at the sight of Mom, who was doing the crossword puzzle in a children's magazine, quite pleased with herself even though Hadley had informed her it was meant for eight-year-olds. The dentist smoothed the front of his shirt and stepped out into the room.

"I'm Dr. Doyle," he said, reaching to shake Hadley's hand, his eyes never leaving Mom, who looked up with a distracted smile.

"Kate," Mom said. "And this is Hadley."

Later, after he'd filled her tooth, Dr. Doyle walked Hadley back out to the waiting area, something her old dentist had never done.

"So?" Mom asked, standing up. "How'd it go? Does she get a lollipop for being good?"

"Uh, we try not to encourage too much sugar here...."

"It's okay," Hadley said, throwing her mom a look. "She's only kidding."

"Well, thanks so much, Doc," Mom said, slinging her purse over her shoulder and putting an arm around Hadley's shoulders. "Hopefully we won't see you again too soon."

He looked stricken by this, until Mom flashed him a too-big grin.

"At least not if we brush and floss regularly, right?"

"Right," he said with a little smile, watching them go.

Months later—after the divorce papers had been filed, after Mom had slipped into some semblance of a normal routine, after Hadley had once again woken up in the night with a sore tooth—Dr. Harrison Doyle finally worked up the nerve to ask Mom to dinner. But Hadley had known even then, that first time; it was something in the way he'd looked at her, with a hopefulness that made the worry Hadley had been carrying around with her feel somehow lighter.

Harrison proved to be as steady as Dad was restless, as grounded as Dad was a dreamer. He was exactly what they needed; he didn't come into their lives with any kind of fanfare, but with a quiet resolve, one dinner at a time, one movie at a time, tiptoeing around the periphery for months until they were finally ready to let him in. And once they did, it was like he'd always been there. It was almost hard to imagine what the kitchen table had looked like when Dad was the one across from them, and for Hadley—caught in a constant tug-of-war between trying to remember and trying to forget—this helped with the illusion that they were moving on.

One night, about eight months after her mom and Dr. Doyle started dating, Hadley opened the front door to find him pacing on their front stoop.

"Hey," she said, pushing open the screen. "Didn't she tell you? She's got her book club tonight."

He stepped inside, careful to wipe his feet on the mat. "I was actually looking for you," he said, shoving his hands in his pockets. "I wanted to ask your permission about something."

Hadley, who was quite sure an adult had never asked her permission for anything before, looked at him with interest.

"If it's okay with you," he said, his eyes bright behind his glasses, "I'd really like to marry your mom."

That was the first time. And when Mom said no, he simply tried again a few months later. And when she said no again, he waited some more.

Hadley was there for the third attempt, perched awkwardly at the edge of the picnic blanket as he got down on one knee in front of Mom, the string quartet he'd hired playing softly in the background. Mom went pale and shook her head, but Harrison only smiled, like it was all some big joke, like he was in on it, too.

"I sort of figured," he said, snapping the box shut again and slipping it into his pocket. He gave the quartet a little shrug, and they kept playing as he settled back onto the blanket. Mom scooted closer to him, and Harrison gave his head a rueful little shake.

"I swear," he said, "I'm gonna to wear you down eventually."

Mom smiled. "I hope you do."

To Hadley, this was all completely baffling. It was like Mom wanted and didn't want to marry him all at once, like even though she knew it was the thing to do, something was holding her back.

"It's not because of Dad, is it?" Hadley had asked later, and Mom looked up at her sharply.

"Of course not," she said. "Besides, if I was trying to compete with him, I'd have said yes, right?"

"I didn't say you were trying to *compete* with him," Hadley pointed out. "I guess I was more wondering whether you're still waiting for him."

Mom took off her reading glasses. "Your father..." she said, trailing off. "We drove each other nuts. And I still don't exactly forgive him for what he did. There's a part of me that will always love him, mostly because of you, but things happened this way for a reason, you know?"

"But you still don't want to marry Harrison."

Mom nodded.

"But you love him."

"I do," she said. "Very much."

Hadley shook her head, frustrated. "That makes absolutely no sense at all."

"It's not supposed to," Mom said with a smile. "Love is the strangest, most illogical thing in the world."

"I'm not talking about love," Hadley insisted. "I'm talking about marriage."

Mom shrugged. "That," she said, "is even worse."

Now Hadley stands off to the side of this little church in London, watching as the young bride and groom emerge onto the steps. Her phone is still pressed to her ear, and she listens to it ring across the ocean, over the wires, around the globe, looking on as the groom's hand searches out the bride's so that their fingers are braided together. It's a small gesture, but there's something meaningful about it, the two of them stepping into the world as one.

When the phone goes to voice mail she sighs, listening to the familiar sound of Mom's voice telling her to leave a message. She finds herself turning around so that she's facing west, almost unconsciously, like it might somehow bring her closer to home, and as she does she notices the narrow point of a steeple just between the white facades of two buildings. Before the phone can beep in her ear she flips it shut again, leaving behind yet another wedding as she hurries in the direction of yet another church, knowing without knowing that this is the one.

When she gets there, rounding a building and then

weaving between the cars parked on either side of the street, she's pulled up short by the scene before her, her whole body going numb at the sight. There on the small patch of lawn is a statue of Mary, the one Oliver used to get in trouble for climbing with his brothers. And standing around it, gathered in tight knots, is a crowd of people wearing shades of black and gray.

Hadley remains rooted a safe distance away, her feet stuck to the sidewalk. Now that she's here, this whole thing seems like the worst possible idea. She knows she's always had a tendency to leap without looking, but she realizes now that this is not the kind of visit you make on a whim. This is not the end point to some spontaneous journey, but rather the site of something deeply sad, something irrevocably and horribly final. She glances down at her dress, the soft purple too cheerful for the occasion, and is already starting to turn away when she catches sight of Oliver across the lawn and her mouth goes dry.

He's standing beside a small woman, his arm resting lightly around her shoulders. Hadley assumes the woman must be his mother, but when she looks closer the scene before her shifts and she realizes it's not Oliver at all. His shoulders are too broad and his hair too light, and when she holds up a hand to shield her eyes from the slanted sun, she can see that this man is much older. Still, she's startled when he looks over, his gaze meeting hers across the yard, and while it's clear now that this is one of Oliver's brothers, there's also something astonishingly familiar in his eyes. Hadley's stomach lurches and she stumbles backward, ducking behind a row of hedges like some kind of criminal.

When she's safely out of sight, hidden to one side of the church, she finds herself just outside a wrought-iron fence woven with vines. On the other side is a garden with fruit trees and a haphazard assortment of flowers, a few stone benches, and a fountain that's cracked and dry. She circles the perimeter, running a hand along the fence—the metal cool to the touch—until she reaches the gate.

Above her a bird cries out, and Hadley watches as it makes lazy circles in the crowded sky. The clouds are thick as cotton and laced in silver from the sun, and she thinks back to what Oliver said on the plane, the word taking shape in her mind: *cumulus*. The one cloud that seems both imaginary and true all at once.

When she lowers her eyes again, he's there across the garden, almost as if she's dreamed him into being. He looks older in his suit, pale and solemn as he digs at the dirt with the toe of his shoe, his shoulders hunched and his head bent. Watching him, Hadley feels a surge of affection so strong that she nearly calls out.

But before she can do anything, he turns around.

There's something different about him, something broken, an emptiness in his gaze that makes her certain this was a mistake. But his eyes hold her there, nailing her to the ground where she stands, torn between the instinct to run away and the urge to cross the space between them.

For a long time they just stay there like that, as still as the statues in the garden. And when he gives her no sign — no gesture of welcome, no indication of need — Hadley swallows hard and comes to a decision.

But just as she turns to walk away she hears him behind her, the word like the opening of some door, like an ending and a beginning, like a wish.

"Wait," he says, and so she does.

13

"What're you doing here?" Oliver says, staring at her as if he's not quite convinced she's actually there.

"I didn't realize," Hadley says quietly. "On the plane..."

He lowers his eyes.

"I didn't realize," she says again. "I'm so sorry."

He nods at the stone bench a few feet away, the rough surface still damp from the earlier rain. They walk over together, heads bowed, the mournful sound of an organ starting up inside the church. Just as she's about to sit, Oliver motions for her to wait, then whips his jacket off and lays it on the bench.

"Your dress," he says by way of explanation, and Hadley glances down at herself, frowning at the purple silk as if she's never seen it before. Something about the gesture cracks her heart open further, the idea that he'd think of something so trivial at a time like this; doesn't he know she couldn't care less about the stupid dress? That she'd gladly curl up on the grass for him, make a bed out of the dirt?

Unable to find the words to refuse him, she sits down, brushing her fingers along the soft folds of his jacket. Oliver stands above her, rolling up first one sleeve and then the other, his eyes focused somewhere beyond the garden.

"Do you need to get back?" Hadley asks, and he shrugs, leaving a few inches between them as he joins her on the bench.

"Probably," he says, leaning forward to rest his elbows on his knees.

But he doesn't move, and after a moment Hadley finds herself pitched forward as well, both of them studying the grass at their feet with unnatural intensity. She feels she probably owes him some sort of explanation for showing up here, but he doesn't ask for one, so they just remain there like that, the silence stretching between them.

Back home in Connecticut, there's a bird bath just outside her kitchen window, which Hadley used to look out at while doing the dishes. The most frequent visitors were a pair of sparrows who used to fight for their turn, one hopping around the edge and chirping loudly as the other bathed, and then vice versa. Occasionally one would dart at the other, and both would flap their wings and lurch backward again, making ripples in the water. But although they generally spent the entire time squabbling, they always arrived together, and they always left together.

One morning she was surprised to see only one of the birds. It landed lightly on the stone lip of the bath and danced around the edge without touching the water, rotating its rounded head this way and that with a sense of bewilderment so pitiful that Hadley had leaned to the window and peered up at the sky, though she knew it would be empty.

There's something of that in Oliver now, a reckless confusion that makes him seem more lost than sad. Hadley's never been this close to death before. The only three missing branches of her own family tree belong to grandparents who died before she was born, or when she was too little to mark their absence. Somehow, she'd always expected this sort of grief to resemble something from a movie, all streaming tears and choking sobs. But here in this garden, there's no shaking of fists at the sky; nobody has fallen to their knees, and nobody is cursing the heavens.

Instead, Oliver looks like he might throw up. There's a grayish tinge to his face, a lack of color that's all the more startling against his dark suit, and he blinks at her without expression. His eyes have a wounded look, like he's been hurt somewhere but can't quite locate the source of the pain, and he pulls in a ragged breath.

"I'm sorry I didn't tell you," he says eventually.

"No," Hadley says, shaking her head. "I'm sorry I just assumed...."

They fall quiet again.

After a moment, Oliver sighs. "This is a little weird, right?"

"Which part?"

"I don't know," he says with a small smile. "You showing up at my father's funeral?"

"Oh," she says. "That."

He reaches down and yanks a few blades of grass from the ground, tearing at them absently. "Really, though, it's the whole thing. I think maybe the Irish had it right, turning it into a celebration. Because this kind of thing"—he jerks his chin in the direction of the church—"this kind of thing is completely mad."

Beside him, Hadley picks at the hem of her dress, unsure what to say.

"Not that there'd be much to celebrate anyway," he says bitterly, letting the pieces of grass flutter back to the ground. "He was a complete arse. No use pretending otherwise now."

Hadley looks up in surprise, but Oliver seems relieved.

"I've been thinking that all morning," he says. "For the last eighteen years, really." He looks at her and smiles. "You're sort of dangerous, you know?"

She stares at him. "Me?"

"Yeah," he says, sitting back. "I'm way too honest with you."

A small bird lands on the fountain in the middle of the garden, and they watch as it pecks at the stone in vain.

There's no water there, only a cracked layer of dirt, and after a moment the bird flies away again, turns into a distant speck in the sky.

"How did it happen?" Hadley asks quietly, but Oliver doesn't answer; he doesn't even look at her. Through the fruit trees lining the fence, she can see people beginning to walk to their cars, dark as shadows. Above them the sky has gone flat and gray again.

After a moment he clears his throat. "How was the wedding?"

"What?"

"The wedding. How did it go?"

She shrugs. "Fine."

"Come on," he says with a pleading look, and Hadley sighs.

"Turns out, Charlotte's nice," she offers, folding her hands in her lap. "Annoyingly nice."

Oliver grins, looking more like the version of himself she met on the plane. "What about your dad?"

"He seems happy," she tells him, her voice thick. She can't bring herself to mention the baby, as if speaking of it might somehow make it so. Instead, she remembers the book, and reaches for the bag beside her. "I didn't return it."

He glances over, his eyes coming to rest on the cover.

"I read a little on the way over," she says. "It's actually kind of good."

Oliver reaches for it, thumbing the pages as he'd done on the plane. "How'd you find me, anyway?"

"Someone was talking about a funeral in Paddington," she says, and Oliver flinches at the word *funeral*. "And I don't know. I just had a feeling."

He nods, gently shutting the book again. "My father had a first edition of this one," he says, his mouth twisting into a frown. "He kept it on a high shelf in his study, and I remember always staring up at it as a kid, knowing it was worth a lot."

He hands the book back to Hadley, who hugs it to her chest, waiting for him to continue.

"I always thought it was only worth something to him for the wrong reasons," he says, his voice softer now. "I never saw him reading anything but legal briefs. But every once in a while, completely out of the blue, he'd quote some passage." He laughs, a humorless sound. "It was so out of character. Like a singing butcher or something. A tap-dancing accountant."

"Maybe he wasn't what you thought...."

Oliver looks at her sharply. "Don't."

"Don't what?"

"I don't want to talk about him," he says, his eyes flashing. He rubs at his forehead, then rakes a hand through his hair. A breeze bends the grass at their feet, lifting the heavy air from their shoulders. From inside the church, the music from the organ ends abruptly, as if it's been interrupted.

"You say you can be honest with me?" Hadley asks after a moment, addressing Oliver's rounded shoulders, and he twists to look at her. "Fine. Then talk to me. Be honest."

"About what?"

"Anything you want."

To her surprise, he kisses her then. Not like the kiss at the airport, which was soft and sweet and full of farewell. This kiss is something more urgent, something more desperate; he presses his lips hard against hers, and Hadley closes her eyes and leans in, kissing him back until, just as suddenly, he breaks away again, and they sit staring at each other.

"That's not what I meant," Hadley says, and Oliver gives her a crooked smile.

"You said to be honest. That was the most honest thing I've done all day."

"I meant about your dad," she says, though in spite of herself, she can feel the color rising to her cheeks. "Maybe it'll help to talk about it. If you just—"

"What? Say that I miss him? That I'm completely gutted? That this is the worst day of my life?" He stands abruptly and, for a brief and frightening moment, Hadley thinks he's going to walk away. But instead, he begins pacing back and forth in front of the bench, tall and lean and handsome in his shirtsleeves. He pauses, spinning to face her, and she can see the anger scrawled across his face. "Look, today? This week? Everything about it has been fake. You think your dad is so awful for what *he* did? At least *your* dad was honest. Your dad had the guts *not* to stick around. And I know that's rubbish, too, but from what it sounds like, he's happy and your mum's happy, and so you're all better off in the end anyway."

All except me, Hadley thinks, but she remains quiet. Oliver begins to walk again, and her eyes follow his progress like a game of tennis, back and forth and back and forth.

"But *my* dad? He cheated on my mum for years. Your dad had one affair, and that turned into love, right? It turned into marriage. It was out in the open, and it set you all free. Mine had about a dozen affairs, maybe more, and the worst part is, we all knew. And nobody talked about it. Somewhere along the line, someone made the decision that we'd all just be quietly miserable, and so that's what we did. But we knew," he says, his shoulders sagging. "We knew."

"Oliver," she says, but he shakes his head.

"So no," he says with a little shrug. "I don't want to talk about my dad. He was a bloody jerk, not just because of the affairs, but in a million other ways, too. And I've spent my whole life pretending it's fine, for my mother's sake. But now he's gone, and I'm done pretending." His hands are balled into fists at his sides, and his mouth is pressed into a thin line. "Is that honest enough for you?"

"Oliver," she says again, setting aside the book and rising to her feet.

"It's fine," he says. "I'm fine."

From a distance comes the sound of his name being called, and a moment later a girl with dark hair and even darker sunglasses appears at the gate. She can't be much older than Hadley, but there's a confidence to her, a sense of ease that makes Hadley feel immediately disheveled by comparison.

The girl stops short when she sees them, clearly surprised.

"It's almost time, Ollie," she says, pushing her sunglasses up onto her head. "The procession's about ready to leave."

Oliver's eyes are still on Hadley. "One minute," he says without looking away, and the girl hesitates, like she might be about to say something more, but then turns around again with a small shrug.

When she's gone, Hadley forces herself to meet Oliver's eyes again. Something about the girl's arrival has broken the spell of the garden, and now she's keenly aware of the voices beyond the hedge, of the car doors slamming, of a dog barking in the distance.

Still, he doesn't move.

"I'm sorry," Hadley says softly. "I shouldn't have come."

"No," Oliver says, and she blinks at him, straining to hear the words inside that word, beneath it or around it: *Don't go* or *Please stay* or *I'm sorry, too.* But all he says is: "It's okay."

She shifts from one foot to the other, her heels sinking into the soft dirt. "I should go," she says, but her eyes say *I'm trying,* and her hands, trembling in an effort not to reach out, say *Please.*

"Right," he says. "Me, too."

Neither of them moves, and Hadley realizes she's holding her breath.

Ask me to stay.

"Good to see you again," he says stiffly, and to her

177

dismay, he holds out a hand. She takes it gingerly, and they hover there like that, halfway between a grip and a shake, their knotted palms swaying between them until Oliver finally lets go.

"Good luck," she says, though with what, she's not entirely sure.

"Thanks," he says with a nod. He reaches for his jacket and slings it over his shoulder without bothering to brush it off. As he turns to cross the garden, Hadley's stomach churns. She closes her eyes against the flood of words that never reached her, all those things left unsaid.

And when she opens them again, he's gone.

Her purse is still on the bench, and as she moves to pick it up again she finds herself sinking down onto the damp stone, folding wearily like the survivor of some great storm. She shouldn't have come. That much is clear to her now. The sun is dipping lower in the sky, and though she has somewhere else to be right now, whatever momentum was propelling her before now seems to have disappeared entirely.

She reaches beside her for the copy of *Our Mutual Friend* and leafs through it absently. When it opens to one of the dog-eared pages, she notices that the corner of the fold reaches halfway down the page like an arrow, its point landing at the top of a line of dialogue: "No one is useless in this world," it reads, "who lightens the burden of it for any one else."

A few minutes later, when she makes her way back past the church, Hadley can see the family still huddled in the open doorway. Oliver's back is to her, his jacket still resting on his shoulder, and the girl, the one who discovered them, stands just beside him. There's something protective about the way her hand rests on his elbow, and the sight of it makes Hadley walk a bit faster, her cheeks reddening without her quite understanding why. She hurries past the pair of them, past the statue with its unwavering gaze, past the church and the steeple and the row of black sedans lined up and ready to lead them to the cemetery.

At the last moment, almost as an afterthought, she places the book on the hood of the car in front. And then, before anyone can stop her, she takes off down the road again.

14

11:11 AM Eastern Standard Time
4:11 PM Greenwich Mean Time

If she were pressed for any sort of specific information about her journey back to Kensington—at what point she switched tubes, who was sitting next to her, how long it took—Hadley would have had a difficult time coming up with answers. To say that the trip was a blur suggests that she could recall at least some of it, no matter how fuzzy, but when she finally steps out into the sunlight again at the Kensington stop, she's struck by the uncomfortable sensation of having skipped through time like a stone.

Apparently, shock—or whatever this is she's feeling—is among the more effective cures for claustrophobia. She's just traveled unseeingly for half an hour, underground the whole time, and not once did she have to force her mind elsewhere. The location was beside the point; her head was *already* in the clouds.

She realizes she left the wedding invitation inside the book, and though she knows the hotel is near the church and therefore somewhere in the neighborhood, she can't for the life of her remember the name. Violet would be appalled.

But when she flips open her phone to call her dad, Hadley notices there's a message, and even before punching in her password she knows it must be from Mom. She doesn't even bother listening, dialing her back right away instead, not wanting to risk missing her yet again.

But she does.

Once more it goes to voice mail, and Hadley sighs.

All she wants is to talk to Mom, to tell her about Dad and the baby, about Oliver and his father, about how this whole trip has been one big mistake.

All she wants is to pretend the last couple of hours never happened.

There's a lump in her throat as big as a fist when she thinks of the way Oliver left her there in the garden, the way those eyes of his—which had studied her so intently on the plane—had been focused on the ground instead.

And that girl. She's absolutely certain it was his ex-girlfriend—the casual way she'd sought him out, the comforting hand on his arm. The only thing she's *not* certain about is the *ex* part. There was something so possessive about the way she looked at him, like she was laying claim to him even from a distance.

Hadley slumps against the side of a red telephone booth, cringing at how silly she must have seemed, seeking him out in the garden like that. She tries not to imagine what they must be saying about her now, but the possibilities seep into her thoughts anyway: Oliver shrugging in answer to the girl's question, identifying Hadley as some girl he met on the plane.

All morning she'd been carrying with her the memory of the previous night, the thought of Oliver acting as a shield against the day, but now it's all been ruined. Even the memory of that last kiss isn't enough to comfort her. Because she'll probably never see him again, and the way they parted is enough to make her want to curl up in a little ball right here on the street corner.

The phone begins to ring in her hand, and she looks down to see Dad's number on the screen.

"Where *are* you?" he asks when she picks up, and she looks left and then right down the street.

"I'm almost there," she says, not entirely sure where exactly *there* is.

"Where you have been?" he asks, and the way he says it, his voice tight, Hadley can tell he's furious. For the millionth time today she wishes she could just go home, but she still has the reception to get through, and a dance with her angry father, everyone staring at them; she still has to wish the couple well and suffer through the cake and then spend seven hours traveling back across the Atlantic beside someone who will not draw her a duck on a napkin, who will not steal her a small bottle of whiskey, who will not try to kiss her by the bathrooms.

"I had to go see a friend," she explains, and Dad grunts.

"What's next? Off to see one of your pals in Paris?"

"Dad."

He sighs. "Your timing could have been better, Hadley."

"I know."

"I was worried," he admits, and she can hear the harshness in his voice beginning to subside. Somehow, she'd been so focused on getting to Oliver that it hadn't really occurred to her that Dad might be concerned. Angry, yes; but worried? It's been so long since he played the role of anxious parent, and besides, he's in the middle of his own wedding. But now she can see how her leaving might have frightened him, and she finds herself softening, too.

"I wasn't thinking," she says. "I'm sorry."

"How long till you get here?"

"Not long," she says. "Not long at all."

He sighs again. "Good."

"But Dad?"

"Yeah?"

"Can you remind me where I'm going?"

Ten minutes later, with the help of his directions, Hadley finds herself in the lobby of the Kensington Arms Hotel, a sprawling mansion that seems out of place amid the crowded city streets, like it was plucked from a country estate and dropped at random here in London. The floors are made of black-and-white marble, alternating like an oversized checkerboard, and there's a great curving staircase with brass railings that stretches up beyond the chandeliered ceiling. Each time someone enters through the revolving doors, the faint scent of cut grass drifts in, too, the air outside heavy with humidity.

When she catches sight of herself in one of the ornate mirrors hanging behind the front desk, Hadley quickly lowers her eyes again. Her fellow bridesmaids will be disappointed when they see that their hard work from earlier has been ruined; her dress is so wrinkled it looks like she's been carrying it around in her purse all day, and her hair—which had been so perfectly styled—is now coming undone, stray wisps falling across her face, the bun in the back sagging badly.

The man behind the desk finishes a phone call, replacing the receiver with a practiced flick of his wrist, and then turns to Hadley.

"May I help you, Miss?"

"I'm looking for the Sullivan wedding," she says, and he glances down at the desk.

"I'm afraid that hasn't yet begun," he tells her with a clipped accent. "It will be held in the Churchill Ballroom at six o'clock sharp."

"Right," Hadley says. "But I'm actually just looking for the groom now."

"Ah, certainly," he says, ringing up to the room and murmuring into the phone before setting it down again and giving Hadley a crisp nod. "Suite two forty-eight. They're expecting you."

"I bet they are," she says, heading toward the elevators.

When she knocks on the door to the suite, she's so busy preparing herself for Dad's disapproving frown that she's a bit surprised to find Violet on the other side instead. Not that there's a lack of disapproval there, either.

"What happened to you?" she asks, her eyes traveling all the way down to Hadley's shoes before snapping back up again. "Did you run a marathon or something?"

"It's hot out," Hadley explains, glancing down at her dress helplessly. She notices for the first time that, in addition to everything else, there's a comma-shaped streak of dirt at the hem. Violet takes a sip of champagne from a glass wreathed in lipstick marks, surveying the damage from over the rim. Behind her, Hadley can see about a dozen people sitting on dark green couches, a tray of colorful vegetables on the table in front of them and several bottles of champagne on ice. There's music playing softly from the speakers, something instrumental and vaguely sleepy, but above that, she can hear more voices around the corner.

"I suppose we'll probably need to sort you out again before the reception," Violet says with a sigh, and Hadley nods gratefully as her phone—which she's still clutching in one sweaty hand—begins to ring. When she glances at the name lit up on the screen, she realizes it's Dad, probably wondering what's taking her so long.

Violet raises her eyebrows. " 'The Professor'?"

"It's just my dad," she explains, so that Violet doesn't

think she's getting strange transatlantic calls from a teacher. But looking down at the phone again, she feels suddenly deflated. Because what had once seemed funny now seems just a little bit sad; even in this—this smallest of gestures, this silliest of nicknames—there's a sort of distance.

Violet steps aside like the bouncer at some exclusive club, ushering Hadley inside. "We don't have much time before the reception," she's saying, and Hadley can't help grinning as she closes the door behind her.

"What time does that start again?"

Violet rolls her eyes, not even bothering to dignify this with a response, and then retreats back into the room, arranging herself carefully on one of the chairs in her wrinkle-free dress.

Hadley heads straight for the small sitting room off to one side, which links the bedroom to the rest of the suite. Inside, she finds her dad and a few other people crowded around a laptop computer. Charlotte is seated before it, her wedding dress pooled all around her like some kind of sugary confection, and though Hadley can't see the screen from where she's standing, it's clear that this is a show-and-tell of sorts.

For a moment she considers ducking back out again. She doesn't want to see photos of them at the top of the Eiffel Tower, or making funny faces on a train, or feeding the ducks at the pond in Kensington Gardens. She doesn't want to be forced to consider evidence of Dad's birthday party at a pub in Oxford; she doesn't need a reminder that she wasn't there, had in fact woken that morning feeling the significance of the day like a weight around her neck, which trailed her through Geometry and Chemistry, all the way through lunch in the cafeteria, where a group of football players had sung a jokey version of "Happy Birthday" to Lucas Heyward, the hapless kicker, and by the end of their awful rendition Hadley had been surprised to discover the pretzel she'd been holding was nothing more than a handful of crumbs.

She doesn't need pictures to know that she's not part of his life anymore.

But he's the first to notice her standing there, her dad, and though Hadley is ready for any number of reactions—anger that she left, annoyance that she's late, relief that she's okay—what she isn't prepared for is this: something behind his eyes laid bare at the sight of her, a look like recognition, like an apology.

And right then, right there, she wishes for things to be different. Not in the way she's been wishing for months now, not a bitter, twisted sort of wish, but the kind of wish you make with your whole heart. Hadley didn't know it was possible to miss someone who's only a few feet away, but there it is: She misses him so much it nearly flattens her. Because all of a sudden it all seems so horribly senseless, how much time she's spent trying to push him out of her life. Seeing him now, she can't help but think of Oliver's father, about how there are so many worse ways to lose somebody, things far more permanent, things that can cut so much deeper.

She opens her mouth to say something, but before the words can begin to take shape, Charlotte beats her to it.

"You're here!" she exclaims. "We were worried."

A glass breaks in the adjacent room and Hadley flinches. Everyone in the sitting area is looking at her now, and the floral-patterned walls seem much too close.

"Were you off exploring?" Charlotte asks with such interest, such genuine enthusiasm, that it twists Hadley's heart all over again. "Did you have fun?"

This time, when she glances in Dad's direction, something in the look on her face is enough to make him stand from where he's been perched on the arm of Charlotte's chair.

"You okay, kiddo?" he asks, his head tilted to one side.

All she means to do is shake her head; at most, maybe shrug. But to Hadley's surprise, a sob rises in her throat, breaking over her like a wave. She can feel her face begin to crumple and the first tears prick the backs of her eyes.

It's not Charlotte or the others in the room; for once, it's not even her dad. It's the day behind her, the whole strange and surprising day. Never has any period of time seemed so unending. And though she knows it's nothing but a collection of minutes, all of them strung together like popcorn on a tree, she can see now how easily they become hours, how quickly the months might have turned to years in just the same way, how close she'd come to losing something so important to the unrelenting movement of time.

"Hadley?" Dad says, setting his glass down as he takes a step in her direction. "What happened?"

She's crying in earnest now, propped up by the doorframe, and when she feels the first tear fall, she thinks—ridiculously—of Violet, and how it's one more thing they'll have to worry about when trying to fix her again.

"Hey," Dad says when he's by her side, a strong hand on her shoulder.

"Sorry," she says. "It's just been a really long day."

"Right," he says, and she can almost see the idea occurring to him, the light going on behind his eyes. "Right," he says again. "Time to consult the elephant, then."

15

Even if Dad still lived at their house in Connecticut, even if Hadley still sat across from him in her pajamas each morning during breakfast and called good night to him across the hall before bed, even then this would still fall under Mom's job description. Absentee father or not, sitting with her as she cries over a boy is absolutely and unequivocally Mom Territory.

Yet here she is with Dad, the best and only option at the moment, the whole story pouring out of her like some long-held secret. He's pulled a chair up beside the bed and is straddling it backward, with his arms resting on the seat back, and Hadley is grateful to see that for once he's not wearing that professorial look of his, the one where he tips his head to the side and his eyes go sort of flat and he arranges his features into something resembling polite interest.

No, the way he's looking at her now is something deeper than that; it's the way he looked at her when she scraped her knee as a kid, the time she flipped her bike in the driveway, the night she dropped a jar of cherries on the kitchen floor and stepped on a piece of glass. And something about that look makes her feel better.

Hugging one of the many decorative pillows from the fancy bed, Hadley tells him about meeting Oliver at the airport and the way he switched seats on the flight. She tells him how Oliver helped her with her claustrophobia, distracting her with silly questions, saving her from herself in the same way Dad once had.

"Remember how you told me to imagine the sky?" she asks him, and Dad nods.

"Does it still help?"

"Yeah," Hadley tells him. "It's the only thing that ever does."

He ducks his head, but not before she can see his mouth move, the beginning of a smile.

There's a whole wedding party just outside the door, a new bride and bottles of champagne, and there's a schedule to keep, an order to the day. But as he sits here listening, it's as if he has nowhere else to be. It's as if nothing could possibly be more important than this. Than *her*. And so Hadley keeps talking.

She tells him about her conversation with Oliver, about the long hours when there was nothing to do but talk, as they huddled together over the endless ocean. She tells him about Oliver's ridiculous research projects and about the movie with the ducks and how she'd stupidly assumed he was going to a wedding, too. She even tells him about the whiskey.

She doesn't tell him about the kiss at customs.

By the time she gets to the part about losing him at the airport, she's talking so fast she's tripping over the words. It's like some sort of valve has opened up inside of her, and she can't seem to stop. When she tells him about the funeral in Paddington, how her worst suspicions had all turned out to be true, he reaches out and places a hand on top of hers.

"I should have told you," she says, then wipes her nose with the back of her hand. "Actually, I shouldn't have gone at all."

Dad doesn't say anything, and Hadley is grateful. She's not sure how to put the next part into words, the look in Oliver's eyes, so dark and solemn, like the gathering of a distant storm. Just beyond the door there's a burst of laughter, followed by scattered clapping. She takes a deep breath.

"I was trying to help," she says quietly. But she knows this isn't entirely true. "I wanted to see him again."

"That's sweet," Dad says, and Hadley shakes her head.

"It's not. I mean, I only knew him for a few hours. It's ridiculous. It makes no sense."

Dad smiles, then reaches up to straighten his crooked bow tie. "That's the way these things work, kiddo," he says. "Love isn't supposed to make sense. It's completely illogical."

Hadley lifts her chin.

"What?"

"Nothing," she says. "It's just that Mom said the exact same thing."

"About Oliver?"

"No, just in general."

"She's a smart lady, your mom," he says, and the way he says it—without a trace of irony, without one ounce of self-awareness—makes Hadley say the one thing she's spent more than a year trying not to say aloud.

"Then why did you leave her?"

Dad's mouth falls open, and he leans back as if the words were something physical. "Hadley," he begins, his voice low, but she jerks her head back and forth.

"Never mind," she says. "Forget it."

In one motion he's on his feet, and Hadley thinks maybe he's going to leave the room. But instead, he sits beside her on the bed. She rearranges herself so that they're side by side, so that they don't have to look at each other.

"I still love your mom," he says quietly, and Hadley is about to interrupt him, but he pushes ahead before she has a chance. "It's different now, obviously. And there's a lot of guilt in there, too. But she still means a lot to me. You have to know that."

"Then how could you—"

"Leave?"

Hadley nods.

"I had to," he says simply. "But it didn't mean I was leaving *you.*"

"You moved to *England.*"

"I know," he says with a sigh. "But it wasn't about you."

"Right," Hadley says, feeling a familiar spark of anger inside of her. "It was about *you.*"

She wants him to argue, to fight back, to play the part of the selfish guy having a midlife crisis, the one she's built up in her head for all these days and weeks and months. But instead, he just sits there with his head hanging low, his hands clasped in his lap, looking utterly defeated.

"I fell in love," he says helplessly. His bow tie has fallen to one side again, and Hadley is reminded that it is, after all, his wedding day. He rubs his jaw absently, his eyes on the door. "I don't expect you to understand. I know I screwed up. I know I'm the world's worst father. I know, I know, I know. Trust me, I know."

Hadley remains silent, waiting for him to continue. Because what can she say? Soon he'll have a new baby, a chance to do it all over again. This time, he can be better. This time, he can be there.

He places his fingers along the bridge of his nose as if trying to ward off a headache. "I don't expect you to forgive me. I know we can't go back. But I'd like to start over, if you're willing." He nods toward the other room. "I know everything's different, and that it will take some time, but I'd really like you to be part of my new life, too."

Hadley glances down at her dress. The exhaustion she's been fighting for hours has started to creep in like the tide, like someone's pulling a blanket up over her.

"I liked our old life just fine," she says with a frown.

"I know. But I need you now, too."

"So does Mom."

"I know."

"I just wish..."

"What?"

"That you'd stayed."

"I know," he says for the millionth time. She waits for him to argue that they're better off this way, which is what Mom always says during conversations like these.

But he doesn't.

Hadley blows a strand of loose hair from her face. What had Oliver said earlier? That her dad had the guts *not* to stick around. She wonders now if that could possibly be true. It's hard to imagine what their life would be like if he'd only just come home like he was supposed to that Christmas and left Charlotte behind. Would things have been better that way? Or would they have been like Oliver's family, the weight of their unhappiness heavy as a blanket over each of them, stifling and oppressive and so very silent? Hadley knows as well as anyone that even the *not saying* can balloon into something bigger than words themselves, the way it had with her and Dad, the way it might have with him and

Mom, had things turned out differently. Were they really better off this way? It was impossible to know.

But what she does know is this: He's happy now. She can see it all over his face, even now, as he sits hunched on the edge of the bed like something broken, afraid to turn and face her. Even now, despite all this, there's a light behind his eyes that refuses to go out. It's the same light that Hadley's seen in Mom when she's with Harrison.

It's the same light she thought she saw in Oliver on the plane.

"Dad?" she says, and her voice is very small. "I'm glad you're happy."

He's unable to hide his surprise. "You are?"

"Of course."

They're quiet for a moment, and then he looks at her again. "Know what would make me even happier?"

She raises her eyebrows expectantly.

"If you'd come visit us sometime."

"Us?"

He grins. "Yeah, in Oxford."

Hadley tries to picture what their house might look like, but can only call to mind some English country cottage she'd probably seen in a movie. She wonders if there's a room for her there, but she can't quite bring herself to ask. Even if there is, it will probably belong to the baby soon anyway.

Before she can answer, there's a knock on the door, and they both look over.

"Come in," Dad says, and Violet appears. Hadley's

amused to see that she's swaying ever so slightly in her heels, an empty glass of champagne in one hand.

"Thirty-minute warning," she announces, waving her watch in their direction. Behind her, Hadley can see Charlotte lean back from where she's sitting in an overstuffed armchair, surrounded by the other bridesmaids.

"No, take your time," she calls to them. "It's not like they can start without us."

Dad glances over at Hadley, then gives her shoulder a little pat as he stands up. "I think we're all sorted in here anyway," he says, and as she rises to follow him out, Hadley catches a glimpse of herself in the mirror, puffy eyes and all.

"I think I might need a little—"

"Agreed," Violet says, taking her by the arm. She motions to the other women, who set down their glasses and scurry over to the bathroom as one. Once they're all huddled around the mirror and everyone's got some sort of tool—a hairbrush or a comb, mascara or a curling iron—Violet begins the round of questioning.

"So what were the tears about, then?"

Hadley would like to shake her head, but she's afraid to move; there are too many people poking and prodding her.

"Nothing," she says stiffly as Whitney hesitates in front of her, a tube of lipstick at the ready.

"Your dad?"

"No."

"Must be tough, though," says Hillary. "Watching him get married again."

"Yeah," Violet says from where she's stooped on the floor. "But those weren't family tears."

Whitney rakes her fingers through Hadley's hair. "What were they, then?"

"Those were boy tears," Violet says with a smile.

Jocelyn is trying to get the stain out of Hadley's dress with a mystifying combination of water and white wine. "I love it," she says. "Tell us all about him."

Hadley can feel herself blushing furiously. "No, it's nothing like that," she says. "I swear."

They exchange glances, and Hillary laughs. "Who's the lucky bloke?"

"Nobody," Hadley says again. "Really."

"I don't believe you for one second," Violet says, then leans down so that her face is even with Hadley's in the mirror. "But I will say this: Once we're through here, if that boy comes within ten feet of you tonight, he won't stand a chance."

"Don't worry," Hadley says with a sigh. "He won't."

It takes only twenty minutes for them to perform their second miracle of the day, and when they're finished Hadley feels like a different person entirely from the one who limped back from the funeral an hour ago. The rest of the bridesmaids stay behind in the bathroom, turning their attention back to their own ensembles, and when Hadley emerges on her own she's surprised to find only Dad and Charlotte in the suite. The others have all returned to their own rooms to get ready.

"Wow," Charlotte says, giving her a finger a little twirl. Hadley spins around obligingly, and Dad claps a few times.

"You look great," he says, and Hadley smiles at Charlotte, standing there in her wedding dress, the ring on her finger throwing off bits of light.

"*You* look great," she tells her, because it's true.

"Yes, but *I* haven't been traveling since yesterday," she says. "You must be completely knackered."

Hadley feels a twang in her chest at the word, which reminds her so sharply of Oliver. For months now, the sound of Charlotte's accent has been enough to kick-start a massive headache. But suddenly it doesn't seem so bad at all. In fact, she thinks she could get used to it.

"I *am* knackered," she says with a weary smile. "But it's been worth the trip."

Charlotte's eyes are bright. "I'm glad to hear that. Hopefully it will be the first of many. Andrew was just telling me you might come for a visit soon?"

"Oh," Hadley says, "I don't know—"

"You *must*," Charlotte says, crossing back into the sitting room, where she grabs the computer again, carrying it out like a tray of appetizers and then sweeping aside a few napkins and coasters to make room for it on the bar. "We'd so love to see you. And we've just renovated. I was showing everyone the photos earlier."

"Honey, is now really the—" Dad starts to say, but Charlotte cuts him off.

"Oh, it'll only take a minute," she says, smiling at Hadley. They stand side by side at the bar, waiting for the images to load. "Here's the kitchen," Charlotte says as the first picture appears. "It looks out over the garden."

Hadley leans in to look closer, trying to spot any remnants of Dad's previous life, his coffee mug or his rain coat or the old pair of slippers he refused to throw out. Charlotte flips from one photo to the next and Hadley's mind races to catch up as she tries to picture Dad and Charlotte in these rooms, eating bacon and eggs at the wooden table or leaning an umbrella up against the wall in the entryway.

"And here's the spare bedroom," Charlotte says, glancing at Dad, who's leaning against the wall a few feet behind them, his arms crossed and his face unreadable. "Your room, for whenever you come see us."

The next photo is Dad's office, and Hadley squints to get a closer look. Though he left all his old furniture behind in Connecticut, this new version looks nearly the same: similar desk, similar bookshelves, even a familiar-looking pencil holder. The layout is identical, though this room looks slightly smaller, and the windows are staggered in different intervals along the two walls.

Charlotte is saying something about the way Dad is so particular about his office, but Hadley isn't listening. She's too busy peering at the framed photos on the walls within the picture.

"Wait," she says, just as Charlotte is about to click through to the next one.

"Recognize them?" Dad says from the other side of the

room, but Hadley doesn't turn around. Because she *does* recognize them. Right there, in the photos within a photo, she can see their backyard in Connecticut. In one of the pictures she spots a portion of the old swingset they've never taken down, the birdfeeder that still hangs just outside his office, the hedges that he always watered so obsessively during the driest of summers. In the other she sees the lavender bushes and the old apple tree with its twisted branches. When he sits in the leather chair at his new desk and looks at the photos, it must seem like he's home again, gazing out a different set of windows entirely.

All of a sudden, Dad is beside her.

"When did you take these?"

"The summer I left for Oxford."

"Why?"

"Because," he says quietly. "Because I always loved watching you play out the windows. And I couldn't imagine getting any work done in an office without them."

"They're not windows, though."

Dad smiles. "You're not the only one who copes by imagining things," he says, and Hadley laughs. "Sometimes I like to pretend I'm back home again."

Charlotte, who has been watching them with a look of great delight, turns her attention back to the computer, where she zooms in on the photo so that they can see a close-up of the frames. "You have a beautiful garden," she says, pointing at the tiny pixelated lavender bushes on the screen.

Hadley moves her finger a few centimeters over, to the

actual window, which looks out over a small yard with a few rows of flowering plants. "You do, too," she says, and Charlotte smiles.

"I hope you'll get to see it for yourself one day soon."

Hadley glances back at Dad, who gives her shoulder a squeeze.

"Me, too," she says.

16

Later, toward the end of the cocktail hour, the doors to the ballroom are thrown open, and Hadley pauses just inside, her eyes wide. Everything is silver and white, with lavender flowers arranged in oversized glass vases on the tables. There are ribbons on the backs of the chairs, and a four-tiered cake topped with a tiny bride and groom. The crystals on the chandeliers seem to catch the light from the silverware, from the gleaming plates and the tiny glowing candles and the brassy instruments of the band, which will sit propped in their stands until later, when it's time for the dancing to begin. Even the photographer, who has walked in just ahead of Hadley, lowers her camera to look around with an air of approval.

There's a string quartet playing softly off to one side, and the waiters in bow ties and tails seem almost to glide through the room with their trays of champagne. Monty winks at Hadley when he catches her taking a glass.

"Not too many," he says, and she laughs.

"Don't worry, my dad will be down to tell me the same thing soon enough."

Dad and Charlotte are still upstairs, waiting to make their grand entrance, and Hadley has spent the entire cocktail hour answering questions and making small talk. Everyone seems to have a story about America, how they're dying to see the Empire State Building (does she go there often?), or planning a big trip to the Grand Canyon (can she recommend things to do there?), or have a cousin who just moved to Portland (does she maybe know him?).

When they ask about her trip to London, they seem disappointed that she hasn't seen Buckingham Palace or visited the Tate Modern or even shopped along Oxford Street. Now that she's here, it's hard to explain why she chose to come for just the weekend, though only yesterday—only this morning, really—it had seemed important that she get in and out as fast as possible, like she was robbing a bank, like she was fleeing for her life.

An older man who turns out to be the head of her dad's department at Oxford asks about her flight over.

"I missed it, actually," she tells him. "By four minutes. But I caught the next one."

"What bad luck," he says, running a hand over his whitened beard. "Must have been quite an ordeal."

Hadley smiles. "It wasn't so bad."

When it's almost time to sit down for dinner, she searches the name cards to find out where she's been placed.

"Don't worry," Violet says, stepping up beside her. "You're not at the children's table or anything."

"What a relief," says Hadley. "So where am I?"

Violet gives the table a scan, then hands over her card. "At the cool kids' table," she says, grinning. "With me. And the bride and groom, of course."

"Lucky me."

"So, are you feeling better about everything?"

Hadley raises her eyebrows.

"Andrew and Charlotte, the wedding..."

"Ah," she says. "I am, actually."

"Good," Violet says. "Because I'll expect you to come back over when Monty and I get married."

"Monty?" Hadley asks, staring at her. She tries unsuccessfully to recall if she's even seen them speak to each other. "You guys are engaged?"

"Not yet," Violet says as she starts walking toward the dining room. "But don't look so gobsmacked. I've got a good feeling about it."

Hadley falls into step beside her. "That's it? A good feeling?"

"That's it," she says. "I think it's meant to be."

"I'm pretty sure it doesn't work that way," Hadley says with a frown, but Violet only smiles.

"What if it does?"

Inside the ballroom, the guests have started to take their seats, tucking purses under chairs and admiring the floral arrangements. As they slip into their places, Hadley notices Violet smiling at Monty across the table, and he gazes back at her for a beat too long before ducking his head again. The band is keying up, the occasional stray note escaping from the trumpet, and the waiters are circulating with bottles of wine. When the motion of the room has slowed, the band leader adjusts the mike and clears his throat.

"Ladies and gentleman," he says, and already the rest of the people at her table—Charlotte's parents and her aunt Marilyn, plus Monty and Violet—are turning toward the entrance to the room. "I'm pleased to be the first to present Mr. and Mrs. Andrew Sullivan!"

A great cheer goes up and there are a series of bright flashes as everyone attempts to capture the moment on camera. Hadley swivels in her seat and rests her chin on the back of the chair as Dad and Charlotte appear in the doorway, their hands clasped together, both of them smiling like movie stars, like royalty, like the little couple on top of the cake.

Mr. and Mrs. Andrew Sullivan, Hadley thinks, her eyes bright as she watches Dad raise his arm so that Charlotte can do a little twirl, her dress fluttering at the bottom. The song is unfamiliar, something just lively enough for them to attempt a little footwork once they've made it to the wooden dance floor in the center of the room, but nothing too fancy. Hadley wonders what significance it might have for them. Was it playing the day they met? The first time they kissed? The day Dad told Charlotte he'd decided to stay in England for good?

The whole place is transfixed by the couple on the floor—the way they lean into each other, laughing each time they pull apart again—yet they might as well be dancing in an empty room. It's as if nobody is watching at all; there's something utterly unselfconscious about the way they're looking at each other. Charlotte smiles into Dad's shoulder, pressing her face close, and he readjusts his hand on hers, twining their fingers together. Everything about them simply seems to fit, and they're practically incandescent beneath the gold-tinged lighting, whirling and gliding beneath the gaze of an entire room.

When the song comes to an end, everyone claps and the bandleader calls for the rest of the wedding party to join them on the dance floor. Charlotte's parents rise from their seats, her aunt is joined by a man from the next table, and Hadley's surprised to see Monty offer a hand to Violet, who grins back at her as they walk off together.

One by one they make their way to the center of the room, until the dance floor is dotted by lavender dresses and the bride and groom are lost in the middle of it. Hadley sits alone at the table, mostly relieved not to be out there but unable to ignore the small stab of loneliness that comes over her. She twists her napkin in her hands as the waiter drops a roll on her bread plate. When she looks up again, Dad is standing beside her, a hand outstretched.

"Where's your wife?" she asks.

"I pawned her off."

"Already?"

He grins and grabs Hadley's hand. "Ready to cut a rug?"

"I'm not sure," she says as he half drags her toward the middle of the room, where Charlotte—who is now dancing with her father—flashes them a smile. Nearby, Monty is doing some sort of jig with Violet, whose head is thrown back in laughter.

"My dear," Dad says, offering a hand, which Hadley takes.

He spins them in a few jokey circles before slowing down again, and they move in awkward rotations, their steps boxy and ill-timed.

"Sorry," he says when he steps on Hadley's toe for the second time. "Dancing has never really been my forte."

"You looked pretty good with Charlotte."

"It's all her," he says with a smile. "She makes me look better than I am."

They're both quiet for a few beats, and Hadley's eyes rove around the room. "This is nice," she says. "Everything looks beautiful."

" 'Cheerfulness and contentment are great beautifiers.' "

"Dickens?"

He nods.

"You know, I finally started *Our Mutual Friend*."

His face brightens. "And?"

"Not bad."

"Good enough to finish?" he asks, and Hadley pictures the book where she left it, on the hood of the black car in front of Oliver's church.

"Maybe," she tells him.

"You know, Charlotte was thrilled when you said you might come visit," Dad says quietly, his head bent low. "I hope you'll actually consider it. I was thinking maybe at the end of the summer, before school starts up again. We've got this spare bedroom that we could make yours. Maybe you could even bring some of your things and leave them here, so that it would seem more like a real room, and—"

"What about the baby?"

Dad drops his arms to his sides and takes a step backward, staring at her with a look of such surprise that all of a sudden Hadley isn't nearly as certain about what she heard earlier. The song ends, but even before the last notes have trailed out over the ballroom, the band rolls straight into the next one, something loud and full of tempo. The tables begin to empty as everyone crowds onto the floor, leaving the waiters to serve plates of salad to vacant chairs. All around them the guests begin to dance, twisting and laughing and hopping around with no particular regard for rhythm. And in the midst of it all, Hadley and her dad stand absolutely still.

"What baby?" he asks, his words measured and deliberate, as if he is speaking to a very small child.

Hadley glances around wildly. A few yards away, Charlotte is peering around Monty, clearly wondering why they're just standing there.

"I heard something back at the church," Hadley starts to explain. "Charlotte said something, and I thought—"

"To you?"

"What?"

"She said something to you?"

"No, to the hairdresser. Or makeup artist. Somebody. I just overheard."

His face loosens visibly, the lines around his mouth going slack.

"Look, Dad," she says. "It's okay. I don't mind."

"Hadley—"

"No, it's fine. I mean, I wouldn't expect you to call and tell me or anything. I know it's not like we talk a lot. But I just wanted to say that I'd like to be there."

He'd been about to say something, but now he stops and stares at her.

"I don't want to miss out anymore," Hadley says in a rush. "I don't want the new baby to grow up thinking of me like some long-lost second cousin or something. Someone you never see, and then instead of going shopping together or asking advice or even fighting, you end up just being really polite and having nothing to say because you don't know each other, not really, not the way brothers and sisters do. And so I want to be there."

"You do," Dad says, but it's not a question. It's insistent, even hopeful, like a wish he's been holding back for too long.

"I do."

The song changes once again, scaling back into something slower, and the people around them start drifting toward their tables, where the salads have all been served. Charlotte reaches out and gives Dad's arm a little squeeze as she walks by, and Hadley's grateful that she knows enough not to interrupt them right now.

"And Charlotte's not so bad, either," Hadley admits, once she's passed.

Dad looks amused. "I'm glad you feel that way."

They're alone now on the dance floor, just standing there while the rest of the room looks on. Hadley hears the clinking of glasses and the clatter of silverware as people begin to eat, but she's still keenly aware that all the attention is still focused on them.

After a moment, Dad lifts his shoulders. "I don't know what to say."

A new thought strikes Hadley now, something that hasn't occurred to her before. She says it slowly, her heart banging around in her chest: "You don't want me to be part of it."

Dad shakes his head and takes a small step closer, putting his hands on her shoulders, forcing her to look at him. "Of course I want that," he says. "There's nothing I want more. But Hadley?"

She raises her eyes to meet his.

"There's no baby."

"What?"

"There will be," he says almost shyly. "Someday. At least we hope so. Charlotte's worried because there's some family history of trouble with these things and she's not as young as, well, your mom was. But she wants it desperately, and the truth is, so do I. So we're hoping for the best."

"But Charlotte said—"

"It's just the way she is," he tells her. "She's one of those people who talks a lot about something when they really want it to happen. It's almost like she tries to will it into being."

Hadley can't help herself; she makes a face. "How's that working out for her?"

Dad grins and waves a hand at the room. "Well, she used to talk about me a lot. And now look at us."

"I'm guessing that was more you than the universe."

"True," he says ruefully. "But either way, whenever we *do* have a baby, I promise you'll be the first to know."

"Really?"

"Of *course*. Hadley, come on."

"I just figured since you've got all these new people over here..."

"Come on, kiddo," he says again, his face breaking into a smile. "You're still the most important thing in my life. And besides, who else can I ask to babysit and change nappies?"

"Diapers," Hadley says, rolling her eyes. "They're called diapers, Dad."

He laughs. "You can call them whatever you want, as

long as you'll be there to help me change them when the time comes."

"I will," she says, surprised to find that her voice is a little wobbly. "I'll be there."

She's not sure what else there is to say after that; part of her wants to hug him, to fling herself into his arms the way she used to as a kid. But all this seems beyond her right now; she's still shell-shocked by the pure momentum of it all, the sheer amount of ground covered in a single day after so much time spent standing still.

Dad seems to understand this, because he's the first to move, slinging an arm around her shoulders to steer her back toward their table. Tucked beside him like that, in the same way she's been a thousand times before—walking to the car together after a soccer game, or leaving the Girl Scouts' annual father-daughter dance—Hadley realizes that even though everything else is different, even though there's still an ocean between them, nothing *really* important has changed at all.

He's still her dad. The rest is just geography.

17

In the same way that Hadley's claustrophobia often manages to shrink even the biggest spaces, something about the reception—the music or the dancing, or even just the champagne—makes the hours seem as if they're no more than a handful of minutes. It's like one of those montages in the movies where everything is sped up, scenes turned into snapshots, conversations into mere instants.

During dinner, Monty and Violet both make their toasts—his punctuated by laughter, hers by tears—and Hadley watches Charlotte and Dad as they listen, their eyes shining. Later, after the cake has been cut and Charlotte has managed to duck Dad's attempts to get even for the white frosting she smeared on his nose, there's more dancing. By the time coffee is served they're all slumped at the table together, their cheeks flushed and their feet sore. Dad sits wedged between Hadley and Charlotte, who— between sips of champagne and tiny bites of cake—keeps flashing him looks.

"Do I have something on my face?" he asks eventually.

"No, I'm just hoping everything's okay with you two," she admits. "After your discussion out on the dance floor."

"That looked like a discussion?" Dad says with a grin. "It was supposed to be a waltz. Did I get the steps wrong?"

Hadley rolls her eyes. "He stomped on my toes at least a dozen times," she tells Charlotte. "But other than that, we're fine."

Dad's mouth falls open in mock anger. "There's no *way* it was more than twice."

"Sorry, darling," Charlotte says. "I'll have to side with Hadley on this one. My poor bruised toes speak for themselves."

"Married only a few hours, and already you're disagreeing with me?"

Charlotte laughs. "I promise I'll be disagreeing with you till death us do part, my dear."

Across the table, Violet raises her glass and then taps it gently with her spoon, and amid the more frantic clinking that follows, Dad and Charlotte lean in for yet another kiss, separating only after realizing there's a waiter hovering just behind them, waiting to take their plates.

Once her own place setting is cleared, Hadley pushes

back her chair and leans forward to pick up her purse. "I think I might go get some fresh air," she announces.

"Are you feeling all right?" Charlotte asks, and Monty winks at her from over the top of his champagne glass, as if to say he'd warned her not to drink too much.

"I'm fine," Hadley says quickly. "I'll be back in a few minutes."

Dad leans back in his chair with a knowing smile. "Say hello to your mom for me."

"What?"

He nods at her purse. "Tell her I said hi."

Hadley grins sheepishly, surprised to have been figured out so easily.

"Yup, I've still got it," he says. "The parental sixth sense."

"You're not as smart as you think you are," Hadley teases him, then turns to Charlotte. "You'll be better at it. Trust me."

Dad slips an arm around his new wife's shoulders and smiles up at Hadley. "Yes," he says, kissing the side of Charlotte's head. "I'm sure she will."

As she walks away, Hadley can already hear Dad beginning to regale his tablemates with stories of her childhood, all the many times he came to the rescue, all the instances when he was a step ahead. She turns around once, and when he sees her he pauses—his hands raised in midair, as if demonstrating the size of a fish or the length of a field, or some other token fable from the past—and gives her a wink.

Just outside the doors to the ballroom, Hadley pauses for a moment herself, standing with her back to the wall. It's like emerging from a dream, seeing the rest of the hotel guests in their jeans and sneakers, the world muted by the lingering music in her ears, everything too bright and slightly unreal. She makes her way through the revolving doors and takes a deep breath once she steps outside, welcoming the cool air and the insistent breeze.

There are stone steps that span the length of the hotel, ridiculously grand, like the entrance to a museum, and Hadley moves off to the side and finds a place to sit down. The moment she does, she realizes her head is pounding and her feet are throbbing. Everything about her feels heavy, and once again she tries to remember the last time she slept. When she squints at her watch, attempting to calculate what time it is back home and how long she's been awake, the numbers blur in her head and refuse to cooperate.

There's another message from Mom on her phone, and Hadley's heart leaps at the sight of it. It feels like they've been apart for much longer than a day, and though she has no idea what time it is at home, Hadley dials and closes her eyes as she listens to the hollow sound of the ringing.

"*There* you are," Mom says when she picks up. "That was some game of phone tag."

"Mom," Hadley mumbles, resting her forehead in her hand. "*Seriously.*"

"I've been dying to talk to you," Mom says. "How are you? What time is it there? How's it all going?"

Hadley takes a deep breath, then wipes her nose. "Mom, I'm really sorry about what I said to you earlier. Before I left."

"It's okay," she says after a half beat of silence. "I know you didn't mean it."

"I didn't."

"And listen, I've been thinking...."

"Yeah?"

"I shouldn't have made you go. You're old enough to make these kinds of decisions on your own now. It was wrong of me to insist."

"No, I'm glad you did. It's been surprisingly...okay."

Mom lets out a low whistle. "Really? I would've bet money that you'd be calling me demanding to come home on an earlier flight."

"Me, too," Hadley says. "But it's not so bad."

"Tell me everything."

"I will," she says, stifling a yawn. "But it's been a really long day."

"I bet. So just tell me this for now: How's the dress?"

"Mine or Charlotte's?"

"Wow," Mom says, laughing. "So she's graduated from *that British woman* to just *Charlotte*, huh?"

Hadley smiles. "Guess so. She's actually sort of nice. And the dress is pretty."

"Have you and your dad been getting along?"

"It was touch-and-go earlier, but now we're fine. Maybe even good."

"Why, what happened earlier?"

"It's another long story. I sort of ducked out for a while."

"You left?"

"I had to."

"I bet your father loved that. Where'd you go?"

Hadley closes her eyes and thinks of what Dad said about Charlotte earlier, about how she talks about the things that she hopes might come true.

"I met this guy on the plane."

Mom laughs. "Now we're talking."

"I went to go find him, but it was sort of a disaster, and now I'll never see him again."

There's silence on the other end, and then Mom's voice comes back a bit softer. "You never know," she says. "Look at me and Harrison. Look what a hard time I've given him. But no matter how many times I've pushed him away, he always comes back around again. And I wouldn't want it any other way."

"This is a little bit different."

"Well, I can't wait to hear all about it when you get back."

"Which is tomorrow."

"Right," she says. "Harrison and I will meet you at the baggage claim."

"Like a lost sock."

"Oh, honey," Mom jokes. "You're more like a whole suitcase. And you're not lost."

Hadley's voice is very small. "What if I am?"

"Then it's just a matter of time before you get found."

The phone beeps twice, and she holds it away from her ear for a moment. "I'm about to run out of batteries," she says when she brings it back.

"You or your phone?"

"Both. So what are you doing without me tonight?"

"Harrison wants to take me to some silly baseball game. He's been buzzing about it all week."

Hadley sits up straighter. "Mom, he's gonna ask you to marry him again."

"What? No."

"Yeah, he totally is. I bet he'll even put it up on the scoreboard or something."

Mom groans. "No way. He'd never do that."

"Yeah, he would," Hadley says, laughing. "That's exactly the sort of thing he'd do."

They're both giggling now, neither of them able to complete a sentence between fits of laughter, and Hadley gives herself over to it, blinking back tears. It feels wonderful, this letting go; after a day like this, she's grateful for any excuse to laugh.

"Is there anything cheesier?" Mom asks finally, catching her breath.

"Definitely not," Hadley says, then pauses. "But Mom?"

"Yeah?"

"I think you should say yes."

"*What?*" Mom says, her voice a few octaves too high.

"What happened? You go to one wedding and all of a sudden you're Cupid?"

"He loves you," Hadley says simply. "And you love him."

"It's a little bit more complicated than that."

"It's not, actually. All you have to do is say yes."

"And then live happily ever after?"

Hadley smiles. "Something like that."

The phone beeps again, this time more urgently.

"We're almost out of time," she says, and Mom laughs again, but this time, there's something weary about it.

"Is that a hint?"

"If it will help convince you to do the right thing."

"When did you get so grown-up?"

Hadley shrugs. "You and Dad must have done a good job."

"I love you," Mom says quietly.

"I love you, too," Hadley says, and then, almost as if they'd planned it, the line goes dead. She sits there like that for another minute or so, and then lowers the phone and stares out at the row of stone houses across the road.

As she watches, a light goes on in one of the upstairs windows, and she can see the silhouette of a man tucking his son into bed, pulling up the covers and then leaning to kiss him on the forehead. Just before leaving the room, the man moves his hand to the wall to flick the light switch, and the room goes dark again. Hadley thinks of Oliver's story and wonders if this boy might need a night-light, too, or whether the good-night kiss from his father is enough to send him off into sleep, a sleep without bad dreams or nightmares, without monsters or ghosts.

She's still watching the darkened window, gazing at the little house in a row of many, past the glowing streetlamps and the rain-dusted mailboxes, past the horseshoe of a driveway leading up to the hotel, when her own sort of ghost appears.

She's as surprised to see him as he must have been when she showed up at the church earlier, and something about his sudden and unexpected arrival throws her off-balance, sets her stomach churning, takes what little composure she has left and shatters it completely. He approaches slowly, his dark suit nearly lost to the surrounding shadows until he steps into the pool of light cast by the hotel lanterns.

"Hi," he says when he's close enough, and for the second time this evening, Hadley begins to cry.

18

6:24 PM Eastern Standard Time
11:24 PM Greenwich Mean Time

A man walks up with his hat in his hands. A woman walks up in a pair of outrageously tall boots. A young boy walks up with a handheld video game. A mother with a crying baby. A man with a mustache like a broom. An elderly couple with matching sweaters. A boy in a blue shirt with not a single crumb from a doughnut.

There are so many ways it could all have turned out differently.

Imagine if it had been someone else, Hadley is thinking, her heart rattling at the idea of it.

But here they are:

A boy walks up with a book in his hands.

A boy walks up with a crooked tie.

A boy walks up and sits down beside her.

There's a star in the sky that refuses to stay put, and Hadley realizes it's actually a plane, that just last night, that star was them.

Neither of them speaks at first. Oliver sits a few inches away, looking straight ahead as he waits for her to finish crying, and for that alone Hadley is grateful, because it feels like a kind of understanding.

"I think you forgot something," he says eventually, tapping the book in his lap. When she doesn't respond, only wipes her eyes and sniffles, he finally turns to look at her. "Are you okay?"

"I can't believe how many times I've cried today."

"Me, too," he says, and she feels immediately awful, because of course he has more right to cry than anyone.

"I'm sorry," she says quietly.

"Well, it's not like we had no warning," he says with a little smile. "Everyone's always telling you to bring a handkerchief to weddings and funerals."

In spite of herself, Hadley laughs. "I'm pretty sure nobody has ever suggested a handkerchief to me in my life," she says. "Kleenex, maybe."

They fall silent again, but it's not strained as it was earlier, at the church. A few cars drive up to the hotel entrance, the tires grumbling, the lights sweeping over them so that they're forced to squint.

"Are you okay?" Hadley asks, and he nods.

"I will be."

"Did it go all right?"

"I suppose so," he says. "For a funeral."

"Right," Hadley says, closing her eyes. "Sorry."

He turns toward her, just slightly, his knee brushing up against hers. "I'm sorry, too. All that stuff I said about my father..."

"You were upset."

"I was angry."

"You were sad."

"I was sad," he agrees. "I still am."

"He was your dad."

Oliver nods again. "Part of me wishes I could've been more like you. That I'd had the nerve to tell him what I thought before it was too late. Maybe then things would have been different. All those years of not talking..." He trails off, shaking his head. "It just seems like such a waste."

"It's not your fault," Hadley says, glancing over at him. It occurs to her that she doesn't even know how Oliver's dad died, though it must have been sudden. "You should've had more time with him."

Oliver reaches up to loosen his tie. "I'm not sure that would have made a difference."

"It would have," she insists, her throat thick. "It's not fair."

He looks away, blinking hard.

"It's like with the night-light," she says, and even when he starts to shake his head, she pushes on. "Maybe the point of the story isn't that he wouldn't help at first. Maybe it's that he came around in the end." She says this last part softly: "Maybe you both just needed more time to come around."

"It's still there, you know," Oliver says after a moment. "The night-light. They turned my room into a guestroom after I left for school, and most of my things are up in the attic. But I noticed it there this morning when I dropped off my bags. I bet it doesn't even work anymore."

"I bet it does," she says, and Oliver smiles.

"Thanks."

"For what?"

"This," he says. "The rest of my family is home, but I felt like I couldn't breathe there. I just needed some fresh air."

Hadley nods. "Me, too."

"I just needed…" he trails off again, glancing over at her. "Is it okay that I'm here?"

"Of course," she says, a bit too quickly. "Especially after I…"

"After you what?"

"Barged into the funeral earlier," she says, wincing a little at the memory. "Not that you didn't already have company."

He frowns at his shoes for a moment before it seems to click. "Oh," he says. "That was just my ex-girlfriend. She knew my dad. And she was worried about me. But she was only there as a family friend. Really."

Hadley feels a quick rush of relief. She hadn't realized just how powerfully she'd wished for this to be true until now. "I'm glad she could be there," she tells him truthfully. "I'm glad you had someone."

"Yes, though *she* didn't leave me with any reading material," he says, thumping a hand against the book.

"Yeah, but she also probably didn't force you to talk to her."

"Or tease me about my accent."

"Or show up without an invitation."

"That'd be both of us," he reminds her, glancing over his shoulder at the entrance to the hotel, where a bellhop is watching them warily. "Why aren't you inside, anyway?"

Hadley shrugs.

"Claustrophobic?"

"No, actually," she says. "It hasn't been too bad."

"You've been imagining the sky, then?"

She looks at him sideways. "I've been thinking about it all day."

"Me, too," Oliver says, tipping his head back.

Somehow, almost without even realizing it, they've moved closer together on the steps, so that although they're not quite leaning against each other, it would be difficult to fit anything between them. There's a scent of rain in the air, and the men smoking cigarettes nearby stub them out and head back inside. The bellhop peers up at the sky from beneath the brim of his cap, and the breeze makes the awning shudder and flap as if it were trying to take flight.

A fly lands on Hadley's knee, but she doesn't move to swat it away. Instead, they both watch it dart around for a moment before it takes off again, so fast they almost miss it.

"I wonder if he got to see the Tower of London," Oliver says.

Hadley gives him a blank look.

"Our friend from the flight," he says with a grin. "The stowaway."

"Ah, right. I'm sure he did. He's probably off to check out the nightlife now."

"After a busy day in London."

"After a *long* day in London."

"The longest," Oliver agrees. "I don't know about you, but the last time I slept was during that stupid duck movie."

Hadley laughs. "That's not true. You passed out again later. On my shoulder."

"No way," he says. "Never happened."

"Trust me, it did," she says, bumping her knee against his. "I remember it all."

He smiles. "Then I suppose you also remember getting into a fight with that woman at the gate?"

Now it's Hadley's turn to look indignant. "I did *not*," she says. "Asking someone to watch your suitcase is a perfectly reasonable request."

"Or a potential crime, depending on how you look at it," he says. "You're lucky I came to your rescue."

"Right," Hadley says, laughing. "My knight in shining armor."

"At your service."

"Can you believe that was only yesterday?"

Another plane crosses the patch of sky above them, and Hadley leans into Oliver as they watch, their eyes trained on the bright dots of light. After a moment, he nudges her forward gently so that he can stand up, then offers her a hand.

"Let's dance."

"Here?"

"I was thinking inside, actually." He glances around—his eyes skipping from the carpeted steps to the restless bellhop to the cars lining up outside the entrance—then nods. "But why not?"

Hadley rises to her feet and smoothes her dress, and then Oliver positions his hands like a professional ballroom dancer, one on her back and the other in the air. His form is perfect, his face serious, and she steps into his waiting arms with a sheepish grin.

"I have no idea how to dance like this."

"I'll show you," he says, but they still haven't moved an inch. They're just standing there, poised and ready, as if waiting for the music to begin, both of them unable to stop smiling. His hand on her back is like something electric, and being here like this, so suddenly close to him, is enough to make her lightheaded. It's a feeling like falling, like forgetting the words to a song.

"I can't believe you're here," she says, her voice soft. "I can't believe you found me."

"You found me first," he says, and when he leans to kiss

her, it's slow and sweet and she knows that this will be the one she always remembers. Because while the other two kisses felt like endings, this one is unquestionably a beginning.

The rain begins to fall as they stand there, a sideways drizzle that settles over them lightly. When she lifts her chin again, Hadley sees a drop land on Oliver's forehead and then slip down to the end of his nose, and without thinking, she moves her hand from his shoulder to wipe it away.

"We should go in," she says, and he nods, taking her hand. There's water on his eyelashes, and he's looking at her like she's the answer to some sort of riddle. They walk inside together, her dress already dotted with specks of rain, the shoulders of his suit a shade darker than before, but they're both smiling like it's some sort of problem they can't shake, like a case of the hiccups.

At the door to the ballroom Hadley pauses, tugging on his hand.

"Are you sure you're up for a wedding right now?"

Oliver looks down at her carefully. "That whole plane ride, you didn't realize my father just died. You know why?"

Hadley isn't sure what to say.

"Because I was with *you*," he tells her. "I feel better when I'm with you."

"I'm glad," she says, and then she surprises herself by rising onto her tiptoes and kissing his rough cheek.

They can hear the music on the other side of the door, and Hadley takes a deep breath before pushing it open. Most of the tables are empty now, and everyone is out on the dance floor, swaying in time to an old love song. Oliver once again offers his hand, and he leads her through the maze of tables, weaving past plates of half-eaten cake and sticky champagne glasses and empty coffee cups until they reach the middle of the room.

Hadley glances around, no longer embarrassed to have so many pairs of eyes on her. The bridesmaids are not-so-subtly pointing and giggling, and from where she's dancing with Monty, her head resting on his shoulder, Violet winks at her as if to say, *I told you so.*

On the other side of the room, Dad and Charlotte have slowed almost to a stop, both of them staring. But when he catches her eye, Dad smiles knowingly, and Hadley can't help beaming back.

This time, when Oliver offers his hand to dance, he pulls her close.

"What happened to those formal techniques of yours?" she says into his shoulder. "Don't all proper English gentlemen dance like that?"

She can hear the smile in his voice. "I'm doing my summer research project on different styles of dancing."

"So does that mean we'll be doing the tango next?"

"Only if you're up for it."

"What are you really studying?"

He leans back to look at her. "The statistical probability of love at first sight."

"Very funny," she says. "What is it really?"

"I'm serious."

"I don't believe you."

He laughs, then lowers his mouth so that it's close to her ear. "People who meet in airports are seventy-two percent more likely to fall for each other than people who meet anywhere else."

"You're ridiculous," she says, resting her head on his shoulder. "Has anyone ever told you that?"

"Yes," he says, laughing. "You, actually. About a thousand times today."

"Well, today's almost over," Hadley says, glancing at the gold-trimmed clock on the other side of the room. "Only four more minutes. It's eleven fifty-six."

"That means we met twenty-four hours ago."

"Seems like it's been longer."

Oliver smiles. "Did you know that people who meet at least three different times within a twenty-four hour period are ninety-eight percent more likely to meet again?"

This time she doesn't bother correcting him. Just this once, she'd like to believe that he's right.

ACKNOWLEDGMENTS

There's a statistical and very probable chance that this book would not have happened without the wisdom and encouragement of JENNIFER JOEL and ELIZABETH BEWLEY. I'm also incredibly grateful to BINKY URBAN, STEPHANIE THWAITES, everyone at ICM and Curtis Brown, the wonderful teams over at Poppy and Headline, my colleagues at Random House, and my very supportive friends and family. Thank you all.

Where stories bloom.

poppy

"*Belles* is a must-read full of scandals, sisterhood, Southern charm, and secrets!"

—Sara Shepard, #1 bestselling author of the Pretty Little Liars series

Two Southern girls. One life-changing secret.

BELLES

Jen Calonita

A new series about what happens when family and friendship collide from the author of the Secrets of My Hollywood Life series, Jen Calonita.

"Will capture readers with its **honesty** and **heart**."

—*Publishers Weekly*

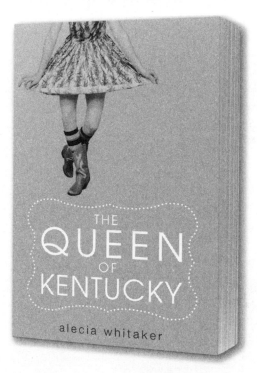

Fourteen-year-old Kentucky girl Ricki Jo Winstead,
who would prefer to be called Ericka, *thank you very much*,
is eager to shed her farmer's daughter roots and become part of
the popular crowd at her small-town high school. But her best friend
and the boy next door, Luke, says he misses "plain old Ricki Jo."

Where does Ricki Jo belong, and
what will it take for her to find out?

poppy
www.pickapoppy.com